Francis and the Animals

Stories by Nic Labriola

Leaping Lion Books
Toronto

Leaping Lion Books
York University, Writing Department
4700 Keele Street
Toronto, Ontario
M3J 1P3

Printed in Canada

First printing, 2013

"Brain Flower" font © Denise Lara Kamille K. Bentulan. Used with permission. All rights reserved.

"Old Dreams" font © Galdino Otten. Used with permission. All rights reserved.

Paperback ISBN: 978-1550145861-1

E-book ISBN: 978-0-9878241-6-5

For my loving mother and father
and generous Anth
and dreaming Miche
and genius Teen
and baby Annie
and for Juna and the moon

Acknowledgments

Special thanks to my father, Tony Labriola, for
his magic in helping me hear and tell these tales.
Thanks to my wonderful mother, and to Anthony,
Michelle, Christina, and Joanna for their laughter
and support. Thanks to Jana for loving animals.
Thanks to Al Moritz for his mentorship. Thanks to
Mike O'Connor and Dan Varrette and the incredible
team at York. Thanks to the kindnesses of those who
helped to *keep off* the madness like Marco, Lori, and
Samantha.
In memory of Stella—the only dog I'll ever love.

Leaping Lion Books Team

Chris Eyles
Paulina Dabrowski
Farrah Abdel Latif
Nicole Brewer
Leah Cann
Francesca Calabretta
Rebecca Campbell
Joshua Cook
Darnell Darby
Andrew de Koning
Rebecca Eade
Frances Gao
Nicole Haldoupis
Stefanie Ioannides

James Karcza
Kyra Kratzmann
Meghan Macivor
Amanda Miceli
Mihai Onufrei
Margaret Puklicz
Jennifer Rawlinson
Cosette Rodriguez
Chelsea Simpson
Jennifer Sipes
Alaina Slavec
Karzan Sulaivany
Isabelle Zerafa

Table of Contents

Tongue

Caught again and doing my best to end things with some nameless bastard with whom I shared a bed. Packing up my clothes into grocery bags, I made it to the front door before he found me, wriggling. He held me by my long, Raggedy-Ann-red hair and forced his fingers inside my mouth. Strangers passed us on the street, unnerved, accustomed to freak shows and hunting in the east end. He almost had me back inside, and I'd already lost my high-heeled black leather boots, kicking, when Constantine arrived. His tongue barely fit inside his mouth. Red blubber emerged from his esophagus and hanging ball in croaking accordion folds that forced him into operatic reptile talk. Indecipherable.

"Lead ear go! Lead ear go! Lead ear go!"

Drooling like a bulldog sucking on a lemon, the tongue popped out and drooped all the way down his chin, quivering like a wet fish, whipping around and smacking against his nose. My boyfriend's rage melted into a puddle by his feet at the sight of it:

disturbed, transfixed, mesmerized. Constantine flexed his wondrous thing and stuck it straight out in front of him like a demon child on a playground. His face was red as a beet and his nostrils flared. Nervous laughter from my boyfriend masked his fear until he coughed a little, whimpered, and went silent. Then he let me go.

But with no place really to go, and on the run since 16 years old, and that final wrestling match with my father that had broken his arm, I followed Constantine's tongue to a tiny room he rented above an ice cream parlour. Through a narrow, slanted, brown-carpeted walk-up, three flights, through a haze of vanilla and burning coconut, he carried my clothes, heavy with each clumping step. Then turning at the door before entering, I think I heard him say, in something like Spanish, "Mi casa es su casa." He had two kind, bulging eyes, pocketed inside his head, that looked like healing stones used to cure the sick.

Inside, the place was decorated with function and luck. Found furniture: a reused table, a patched-up couch, a mismatched mattress and box spring, one king, one queen. The door closed with the weight of my sudden vulnerability. This is how I always enter a man's house. And with the allure of the tongue's rescue fading, I locked myself in the bathroom, without saying a word and stared at the giant rubber duckies on his shower curtain.

I started to search through his medicine cabinet for evidence of serial killings, disorders, kinks, or other addictions. I looked for something to explain his extraordinary mouth, but the toothbrush was normal size, and he used ordinary mouthwash. No strange bits of headgear or elastic devices to accompany such a mutation. I was looking for a wooden spoon that he might sleep with to prevent him from swallowing the bloody thing, but there was nothing.

I pried open a window above the toilet, looked out onto a fire escape. I had slipped through windows before. I climbed onto a radiator, shimmied up, and landed safely on steps lined with wrought iron. Escape was simple for me. I felt as if I'd been born that way and had freed myself at birth from my mother's body and never looked back.

But when I finally made it to street level, I did look back. I saw Tongue going into the ice cream parlour. He was shapeless, grey. A rock that entered the bright purple, orange, and red shop. I crossed the street to avoid being seen. I watched him study a menu behind a counter, banter with a girl wearing a paper hat, sample something

pink from a tiny, wooden spoon. His tongue was more moist and
radiant than the desserts. He bought two waffle cones with cherries
on top and left. Back out on the street, he held them in his meat hooks
as the tip of his tongue worked away. It was like watching a camel
going at a slab of salt. Seeing him that way, a cartoon animal, or even
just an animal, dispelled my fears.

"Hey!" I yelled to him.

"Heee!" He yelled back, not surprised to see me. "Tss cherry!"
And he held out a cone for me.

We ate the cherry ice cream cones on the roof of his building.
Although we were only a few stories up, I was high enough to see
all that I wanted of the city. High enough for someone to commit
suicide and still be able to glimpse the world before landing. We leaned
against a wooden fencing.

"Makes you want to jump," I told him, but he didn't agree.

"Naw, it don't."

"Feels like a giant hand could reach up over the edge, grab me,
and pull me over. And I'd let it pull me over and down, all the way
down, as long as I could watch the crash."

"Naw, it don't," he said again.

"It's like staring at a rushing waterfall. Or like the second before
the subway comes . . . makes you want to jump."

But for him, it didn't. He acted like he hadn't heard me and
continued to lick away like a lizard.

"Ever drop acid?" I asked. "You put it under your tongue and
just let it sit there until it dissolves. It makes you see visions."

"Oh, dreams?" he asked.

"Almost."

Tongue came towards me and stood inches away. Tilting his
medicine ball head back, he closed his eyes and opened up his mouth.
His tongue was a bright flamingo pink now from the ice cream. I placed
a strip inside and took a hit myself. Tongue winced. He clamped his
mouth shut. I heard the molars in his head snap like a trap closing.

"Do I choo?" he asked through clenched teeth. "No taste."

I saw his jaw muscles bulge. Told him to let it melt. He lay
sprawled on the tarred roof like a tranquilized horse waiting to be put
down. His breathing was slow and deep. I was falling under and felt
as if he were sucking in all the air around us. He turned to look at me
and whispered something that sounded like,

"Melting."

My trip took a wrong turn when I heard him howl. Tongue was rigid on his back now, cruciform, staring up at the sky. His piercing cry was neither pleasure, nor pain. I tried shushing him, lulling him back under, because the brute was ruining it for me.

"Melting!" he screamed.

He sprung into action. Took shape out of his shadow on the rooftop. Climbed up over the railing. I went after him, but he had already managed to climb over to the other side. I grabbed him by the back of his belt. Tongue continued to screech and arched his body towards the street. I wasn't going to be responsible for this idiot's death, although in that instant I was convinced his entire body was made of rubber and that if he did plummet, he'd surely just bounce back up like some huge red utility ball.

"Flying!" he continued with outstretched arms. "Lead me go!"

His belt was cutting into my fingers. A small line of blood began to form. I was losing circulation in my arms. With my free hand, I grabbed him by his thick, curly, blonde hair and pulled his head back towards the safety of the ledge. Tongue began to laugh even though I was ripping out his goddamn locks from the roots. His disgusting tongue protruded in spasms from the vibrations of his belly. I reached for it, seized the slimy thing in my right hand, and started to pull. It writhed and slipped in my grip. I dug my nails into the frenulum and dragged it toward me. His massive body followed. He slunk back on top of the roof, mumbling, coughing and chanting:

"Humpity Dumpity sat on a wall. Humpity Dumpity had a great fall."

We must have fallen asleep soon after and spent most of the night up there, but I don't remember how I ended up in his bed the next morning, or if he had spent the night beside me. When I woke up, I was alone staring up at a wrestling poster on the ceiling. The man in the picture had on green and yellow face paint. He was bearing his bottom teeth as if they were fangs. His greasy hair was long and swept back. There were ribbons tied to the bends in his glistening orange arms and legs.

Tongue was puttering away in the kitchen. The previous day's exertion had taken its toll on my body, and I could barely get out of the enormous bed. I heard Tongue singing opera in the other room. I found him hunched over a hotplate, scrambling eggs. A small black and white television played morning cartoons under poor reception.

"Scrambies," he said when he saw me.

I went inside to the bathroom and saw a shipwreck in the mirror. The details of how I'd washed up with this gargantuan chef were unclear. I was in no shape to go to a funeral. I searched my pockets for my father's obituary: *Surrounded by his family, Patrick McKegan passed away peacefully at St. Michael's Hospital on Tuesday. Services will be held Friday at 1 p.m. at Eternal Hope.*

Dearest Daddy's death had not surprised me when I came across it at the back of the newspaper. It was the idea that he had been surrounded by his family that was tough to take. I hadn't seen or spoken to anyone from my clan in eight years, and didn't want to believe that any of them had given him any comfort or forgiveness when he expired.

I tied my hair into a tight ponytail and joined Tongue for breakfast. He had arranged the eggs into a face on my plate. Burnt bacon strips in the shape of a mouth smiled up at me. A blueberry muffin nose.

"Any coffee?" I asked.

"Yuck," said Tongue.

He wore a tight, yellowed wife-beater shirt and baggy, brown cotton pants. Still staring at his television show, he lapped happily at his meal.

"Want to go to a funeral?" I asked him.

"When?"

"This afternoon."

"Don't like eggs?" he asked with a mouth full of bacon.

"Yuck," I said.

Tongue and I went to a Salvation Army store a few blocks away from his house. Neither of us had anything appropriate to wear to the cemetery; although, I didn't know exactly what would be appropriate to wear to the burial of a madman. I knew it wasn't black. The store smelled like mildew; it was a familiar odour. Racks of used clothes sprawled out before us. They reminded me of all the people who must be alive out there, sweating out armpits, outgrowing dresses, ripping the seats of pants, spilling fluids, making stains. A mess.

Tongue wandered off into the back of the place while I started sorting through some of the rotted ruins. I knew my old man would spin in his stinking grave if I showed up to his funeral in a pair of cut off jeans and a halter-top. But if I were to wear something like that, I would only be choosing it because of him—to disgrace him. And if I were to wear something less shocking, if I were to wear black, I'd still only be choosing it because of him. So I was trapped.

Tongue appeared out of nowhere wearing a pair of leather chaps. They didn't fit. He bulged out of them like swollen fruit.

"Cute," I said.

He was pleased and galloped off.

With every item I picked up—every blouse, skirt, jacket, and pantsuit—I couldn't picture myself wearing it without seeing my father's dead eyes leering at me. Devouring me. There was nothing I could put on that he did not have control over. I could never dress myself without first reflecting on how I would appear to him, even now that he was a corpse. So I decided to wear what I had on.

Tongue emerged from the change room in a massive white suit. He was beautiful. The intense ivory draped his powerful body in a way that I did not think was possible because he was so large. I couldn't imagine another man owning and wearing that same suit before Tongue.

"Constantine in gabardine," Tongue said proudly.

Tongue donated his brown pants to the store, paid for his suit, and we left. I was walking beside a white wall. The sun shone through him, penetrated his square shoulders and massive back. It was hard to look at him without squinting. Passing a garden on the way to the cemetery, Tongue found some flowers.

"No way," I said. "No goddamn flowers."

"Not for him," he said.

Tongue ripped out a couple of pink begonias and inserted a stem into the buttonhole of his new jacket. The flower opened up on his lapel, the petals made all the more vivid by the whiteness that surrounded them.

"Well, aren't you pretty," I said.

"You're pretty," he said, and he gave me the other flower to put somewhere on my body. I stuck the thing behind my ear.

"Good enough," he said.

By the time we arrived, the service was already underway. Tongue and I took cover behind a slate grey mausoleum. We sat on its steps. From a distance, I saw a swarming of blue and black bugs around a hole in the earth. Fifteen men huddled together around a shiny box. I knew it was my family because of all the fiery red hair. My cheeks burned thinking about all that wiry orange fur. I began to gag, as if I were swallowing talcum powder. Tongue peeked around the corner and started to laugh. I looked back at them. My brothers and uncles were taking turns pouring whiskey on my father's grave, weeping. I wanted to rip the priest's eyes out.

Tongue went ahead of me and joined the circle of male mourners. He towered over the others. They all looked like headstones to me. Tongue waited patiently for his turn to pour. When it came, he clutched the bottle with both hands and began to sprinkle the whiskey over the casket. My brothers realized that Tongue was misplaced when he wouldn't stop pouring. He was now walking in circles around the grave, lost inside his own ritual.

"That's enough son," the priest said.

But Tongue continued to pour.

"I said that's enough."

My brothers and uncles intervened and tried to grab the bottle away from Tongue. He dodged them, holding onto the bottle, and weaved his way through them until they managed to encircle him entirely. Tongue held the bottle high above their heads. I could no longer see him except for his long arm that emerged high above the group. I could hear him calling to me. I ran over.

Tongue was fighting them off, desperate to keep the bottle from spilling. He managed to knock a few of the men over. The pack opened up, all of them panting, exchanging their tears for rage. That's when they saw me.

Tongue's begonia had been ripped into pieces and his face was seething red, but that white suit was still impeccably white. He freed himself from the remaining hands that held onto him and walked over to me. He handed me the bottle of whiskey, put his arm around my shoulders, and led me to the grave.

I emptied the bottle of booze over my father's box. Then clutching the neck of the bottle, I smashed it against the headstone. Glass shattered and spit into the air. Tongue sprung back from the explosion. I looked down at my hand. Blood mixed with whiskey in my palm. I brought it to my mouth and licked at the small wound with my tongue.

Constantine came too close, eyes crossed, bearing down on me, like a semi hauling a load of love. As if itching for an open-mouthed kiss, itching to stick his tongue down my throat. "Justice for the dead," he said. "Justice for the living."

The Crusade of Miles Free
an urban fable

Miles danced in life, free. He was loved and was
admired because of it. He went at the world with
a kindness and a spirit and a beating heart that no
one had to teach him. Loved life. Played it like an
alto sax. All aspects—the people he'd met and the
places he'd seen—notes in the scale. Everything
went together. Everything fit. There was harmony,
and there was dissonance, and it was always a song.
So when Miles went insane, it troubled the people
around him, as well as those who'd heard about him,
as well those who looked to him for inspiration. The
story of his decline begins on the day he rescued
that bird with the busted-up wing. On that spring
day, it begins.

    Miles hears a fluttering against the back-porch
door. He peeks outside and sees a good-sized sparrow
in spasm, unable to fly. He finds a shoebox, some
blue tissue paper, goes outside, and picks up the
bird. He begins to nurse it. This is Miles nursing the
bird. Feeding it seeds he buys at the store. Keeping

it dry. Keeping the temperature in his house fit for a bird. Naming it. Naming it Lucas. He loves Lucas, the bird. And that bird, in turn, loves Miles Free.

The time comes to see if the care and kindness have paid off. Here they are, saying their goodbyes, packing a lunch, and opening up a window. The sky is a field of blue birds, and the blueness of it pours into the room. Lucas takes the scene in and a deep breath in and hops out onto the windowsill. He braces himself and, unfolding his wings, takes flight.

Miles looks on with that mad rhythm in his heart. Lucas is flying. He does a full turn of the yard, chirping his little bird ass off. Quite the show. The busted-up wing has mended and doubled in power and flutter speed. But before he goes out to face the world beyond Miles' watchful eye, Lucas, the bird, rests a moment on a fence, looks back at Miles, beaks him adieu, and flies. This is Miles flapping his arms like the bird he loves.

What looks like a fur sack—a cat—lunges and catches Lucas full in its mouth. It bites down and disappears into the alleyway with a mess of feathers and blood. Miles sees it in a nightmare flash. Death is a furry, black sack—a cat. He runs outside. The cat is gone. The bird is really gone.

It's all so fast. Too fast. It strikes him hard. Hits him in the gut. Hard. It starts to poison his belly. He feels it push through his body. Feels like his back is over his head. His ears are bleeding from down inside his throat.

This is Miles, turning on the radio, turning it up loud, and wailing like a tenor sax—crying like a baby. He tucks himself in a foetal pose on the ground. He lies on a purple rug with a pink moon in the design, and wild, gold zigzags at its borders. Miles leaves a puddle of himself, tears and snot and wet anger. He lies there and lies there until he finds a way to suck it up. Stand up, he says, and does. Then, whispering a small, almost-prayer for Lucas, the bird, Miles changes for work.

He was a courier. A deliveryman. Miles cruised downtown in a pair of roller skates, hand-delivered documents and blueprints and other legal news to the men and women of Bay Street and beyond. He wore yellow goggles, wore an oxygen mask, wore tight-fitting blue clothes and blue gloves with the fingers cut out. He was good at his job. Fast and efficient. It was good money. He was a natural. It gave him a chance to work with people—new people every day. And the traffic, and the deadlines, and the hot heads, and the paper cuts were never a problem for Miles flying by in his downtown skates. Point A to point B. The stress of that job had suited him well—well up until that particular day.

Miles finds his mind wandering back to the cat's mouth. The death of the bird. Why has it happened? He searches for meaning between assignments.

"New copy's up, Miles. For Crumpecker. Over on Richmond. 11B."

Mad thoughts, like finding that cat and drowning it, parachute in. Wretched thoughts. Miles loves cats. Always has.

"Good to see you, Miles," says the dispatcher. "Tell Andrews to double-check these signatures or it's my ass—his ass too. How've you been anyway? The Bodwell Building, up on 12."

Miles bites his lip until the tooth pierces through to keep his mind off the killing. Keep his memory off. His mind is a sky. His memory, coil-bound with addresses and names and the numbers of floors. Yet he's lost his concentration. He's behind schedule. He starts to resent his all-important role as the middleman. What is it all about? Pieces of paper?

This is Miles lost inside an old factory building that's been converted to offices. The place is enormous. He has some kind of package for someone named somebody on some floor in some room, number three. He's sweating. Wet. Annoyed. Needle in the hay. Grain in the heap. He skates over to a back stairwell and rests.

It's a manila envelope that he carries in his black sack. Lightweight, thin. He sets it down beside him. The corners are crumpled, and he smudges the ink with wet fingerprints. He has no reference point for working out this kind of mishap. He grabs the package, holds it up to the light. There is a single piece of paper inside. He can't make out any words. A vein pops up on his forehead. A river of blood runs clear in his brain. No one is around. Miles tries gently to open the envelope without tearing it. Working away at the sticky fold. Working away in spite of any federal offence, until he just has to tear and rip the damn thing open. Miles shreds. In two, then four, then eight, then sixteen, then thirty-two, then sixty-four, then one-hundred-and-twenty-eight. He stuffs the pieces of the sheet one by one inside of his cat-like mouth—a forced communion. Slobbers on those bits in his mouth. Bites down. Stands up. Leans over the railing, almost gagging, and spits. The stuff flies out. clumped—some pieces free—and showers down on the steps below.

On his lunch break, Miles can't eat—won't eat. A dread wells up inside him. Dread: His job. His life. Ten years of flying up and down Bay Street, dodging cars and pedestrians—why? He feels sick. Sitting on a bench in a parkette, in between buildings, he looks around and is overtaken by waves of emptiness. He counts cars on the road, street lamps, people walking by in nowhere lines, in nowhere circles. They walk in and out of buildings that lift up off the ground to nowhere. He hears sounds of the wind against the smog, against random conversation: *all the way through, the wind was saying, from my pocket if you can believe it. . . for what was about an hour and a half. . . forecast if you must . . . by and by, my friend, by and by . . . definitely a peach for Tuesday's boy . . .* All set against a polluted sky that now seems quite confined with clouds that won't be shaped in his mind's eye.

He is amazed. He'd never noticed it before. Nothing. And the more he looks for purpose, and the more he examines his surroundings for meaning, the closer he comes to empty. So he keeps his eyes wide and takes it all in: sweet nothing, sweet nothingness. Faceless bodies of people. Industry for jobs and transit to travel to make-believe. He is dizzy. Kneeling down on the curb, he undoes his skates, steps out barefoot onto the concrete street. This is Miles on the Earth.

A sewer grate catches his eye. Miles lies flat on the ground against it and looks down. Too dark to see in. What's down there? He looks back out into the street, squints. What's down there? Miles grabs hold of the grate and starts to pull; gets to his feet and pulls; hands aching, pulls; arms extended between his legs, pulls, until the trapdoor gives way and comes off. Miles reels back, amazed at his strength. He tosses the grate aside and, belly down, shimmies into the hole.

His feet secure metal bars going down, down beneath the street until he hits bottom. Light pours in from above. Miles is underground. It's calm down there. Cool down there. He feels protected. Safe. Barefoot. The stink isn't overwhelming. The stink is just fine. He walks through a river of waste and scum with his pant legs rolled up and his eyes fixed straight ahead of him. His heart beats again.

The tunnel underground stretches out for miles—miles of freedom. Yes. The simplicity contained inside of those reeking halls is an unknown city where Miles is a traveller. A pilgrim.

"Hallelujah." A voice comes from the dark tunnel. "My eyes

have seen the wonder and the function of the world." Miles walks and walks until his spirit can't push him any further. Guided by a shadow of moonlight from some far-off opening, Miles finds a comfortable hole inside the concrete. He burrows himself in and falls asleep.

She came to him first in a dream vision, until he woke up and found her wild, real. There she was—in the flesh, he swears—like an angel over him. Bird head and bird wings. Her hair, a mass of tangles, swept over a gaunt face. Her eyes, two large pockets of glass. And her body, almost a collection of bones. On her bones, ghost-skin, blue-veined, veiled in an ancient dress. As worn out and ancient as she was. With her thin mouth, smudged, charcoal-drawn, over his forehead, over his sleepy eyes, over his crusted grimy body—over Miles, over Miles Free. The two of them danced. They danced and danced. They danced and danced underground in that pit—that open sewer—like it was the centre of world and it was.

The sun is coming up over the opening above the concrete. It pours in from cracks and grates and openings from the overhead world. Miles is alive. The woman, like a bird, moves: ageless and broken down and beautiful. Miles swamps after the goddess. But the river deepens, rises waist high, then chest high, then neck, until they are swimming. Moving to a light source. Miles' eyes are drawn to it. To a passage that opens up. The river is flowing, flowing out. The river is becoming an ocean. A current takes over and the two give over. Swept away. Falling out. Busting out of the mouth of that sewer. Out of that river into that ocean.

Miles is deep underwater. He looks up and sees a morning sun past a sky of water in that boundless sky without a top. Sees birds flying in that sky above the sky of water. He emerges and sucks in the air around him. But she is gone. That ancient woman—gone. There is no one around. He calls to her: "Sky. Sewer. Earth. Lover. Life. Death." Miles is lovesick. Miles is heartbroken. Loveless. Pierced through, chewed up, spat out. He comes too close. He goes insane.

The next day and the days that followed were marked by a change in his eyes. In the way he moved, and spoke, and travelled on his roller skates. Or by his visits underground, searching. Or the way he took to eating fruit by the basket. And how he chain-smoked cigarettes, pack after pack. And by the tears that ran wild when he laughed too hard. He no longer danced but spun, whirling through life in a way that people had to call crazy. Friends looked at him strangely, now. His family shook their heads, sighed. But strangers didn't notice a goddamn thing because Miles was still Miles, and Miles was still free. He had just come too close; a little too close to paradise, open and ready like a mouth of an unknown alley cat.

Shooting Penelope

I Named Her Penelope Moon
Heading south on Yonge Street, I was breathing
with my mouth open. The silver sliver of a cracked
moon couldn't compete with the neon burning in
my eyes. I stepped in a big pile of horseshit. Two
Mounties clopped up onto the curb on carousel-
purple Clydesdales, their manes cascading down,
and seemed to paint the concrete orange and red.
Then some pecker-head passerby, wearing a purple
t-shirt, grabbed the attention of one of the two cops
and performed his civic duty.

"There's some crazy girl running up and down
the street knocking things down and moving as if
she's on some kind of upper."

And there she was. I turned on my video
camera to shoot her. Named her Penelope Moon.
She was crossing on a red, and just swerving through
traffic. Behind her, a trail of vandalized potted
plants and store signs, of victimized mailboxes
and toppled newspaper stands. Everything bowled
over and pushed to the ground, the work of some
powerful, rioting wind, rushing by and taking out
any and all things in its way. And this gale force, just

a girl. She came to a standstill by a sweating panhandler who kept his long, greasy hair swept back and parted down the middle. She moved her head back and forth to the drone of her headphones, dancing by a bus stop, waiting for a Blueline to come. I molested her with my stare. Hoping maybe to be swept up by her rage, like a fallen object that had once stood in her way.

She was barely there: her slight body, a slender frame. Her eyes looked like glass, pocketed deep inside her skull; silent film star cheekbones jutted out and so did the ridge of her brow. A Native Marlena Dietrich, her skin, a pale moon glow turning blue. The bus chugged by blowing heavy on a rusted bassoon. It was packed window to window with overgrown insects, nursing hangovers and busted up, still-buzzing wings. When Penelope stumbled and boarded the bus, I was left alone to inhale exhaust fumes, and repeatedly dragged my boot heel off the sidewalk in an attempt to get the horseshit off the sole.

I wanted to sleep. I was already numb, dreaming, going over it, flipping through thoughts and lists of losing control, and perspective. No confidence, or peace—just my eyes wide open, the lenses at the mercy of what was going on. What was going on beyond my outrage at school? A cry of disillusionment and the way personal demons were already plucking out my vile jellies as they often did and taunting me about my looming failure as a filmmaker. I was always laughing inside my head at my one-time feeling of making it, calling myself an artist. My eyes were open, but barely; and judging by the way I was moving down the street, it was sleep, and it wasn't, because I wasn't still, and wasn't lying down.

The Diner
Fell asleep in Queen's Park. My body was soundless on a bench, under a tree, under the moon, dreaming about turning inside out, going from student to monster and back again. Awoke to find myself curled up and sandwiched between the homeless man with the perfect hair and his dog. Warm saliva and a tongue on my eyes, I came to and tried to shoo away a snout burrowing itself into my crotch. I kicked the dog. Fangs retaliated and bit my ankle. Tore my pants and punctured the skin. A love bite inscribed on my heel, teeth marks imprinted in red and blue. Never been bitten before. Not by a dog.

A diner on the corner of Bathurst and Dupont called to me from across the Annex. Not eating or thinking to eat for days, I was starving. I sat down at the long, greasy bar lined with red, plush leather stools. Behind it, a huge stove and fryer sizzled up the meat. The place had been preserved from 1952. The owners were Greek or Italian; old and married, or should have been. I mumbled an order of fries and a coke. Sat hunched on my stool. I was perched like a hungry little bird, waiting to peck and gobble up my meal. A plate and bottle were set down in front me with a bowl of vinegar on the side. I drenched the fries and began to gorge myself.

I was thinking coconut ice cream. Thinking cherry pie. That's what they slid down to me next. Swallowed and imploded a little. I gazed up at the wall across from me and caught my reflection in the glass of a framed map of the city. I saw myself in the foreground: young, dishevelled, bearded. Close-up of me: ugly as hell, with deep lines in my forehead and bags under my eyes. A drooling Neapolitan Mastiff bitch. Penetrating the picture, to see past my dog-face, I traced Penelope's route: her streets in the east end, the shelter on Queen and Jarvis where I'd taken those first few shots of her. Streets in Toronto move from chic to shit-hole and back again with ease. I was starting to understand that that was how she moved, too.

Food sliding down my gut began to travel through and rejuvenate my body. I had to scrounge in my pockets to come up with enough change to pay the bill. Not enough for a tip, though. Never enough.

Leonard

Inside my apartment, removing my boots and shirt, standing half naked in the kitchen, I was a Minotaur with a pierced ankle. Lifted my foot and let cold water from the sink run on the punctures. I towelled off with my t-shirt and stuck my head under the stream. Let the water run cold needles through my hair. It trickled down the back of my neck and spine.

Leaving the faucet, I pressed play on a blinking answering machine. It was Grace. She was sighing in her usual singsong, calling to me, repeating my name again and again—Leonard? Lenny? Len? Len?—until she finally began her message. I couldn't bear to listen. I went back to the running water, pivoted, and opened my mouth. Water filled up and poured into my nostrils. Drowning.

Grace's words played out in the other room, just out of earshot. I could hear them muffled by the tin-tone tone of the machine, as if underwater. I was listening to some distant, shrieking rainforest.

Opening my eyes, I tried to watch the waterfall. It blinded me, until I built up a kind of tolerance for it. The stinging subsided. There was peace, drowning. I could almost bear the pain in my girlfriend's voice. Gasping for air, I bounded back and shook myself off. Water leapt off my wet head and splattered the walls. I ran a dishrag across my chest, then bent down and used it to bind my swelling ankle. Tilting my head to the side, I banged at my temple with the palm of my hand in an attempt to unclog my waterlogged ear.

Luna

Aquamarine shadows cast down from the cinema screen. My hands were cut up into fragments of bone by the light. It hollowed out heads in front of me, elongated lines on the wall. The class was a gash in the garish glow.

I was spellbound as usual, entranced by the moving pictures in Professor Wylie's film theory class. 11 a.m., I'd come late. Missed the first half hour. I was unsure of the title. I didn't know if the naked woman on the screen called Luna was speaking Italian or French, and I didn't care. All I understood was the erection in my pants.

Students were scribbling down lecture notes all around me, as if they were composing a last will and testament. I stuffed my right hand inside my pocket and tried to let the film absorb me as I always want films to do. Each frame could block out life's troubles, if only for a couple of hours in the dark, dismissing the mundane and commonplace—the pathetic worries of a twenty-something university student with eyes most of the time rolled back in his head. I was searching and scratching for a glimpse of my own mind, or anyone else's.

A wide-angle crane shot of the Eiffel Tower let me know that I was, in fact, in France. Luna and a guy with a trimmed beard were driving in a scenic countryside in a retro VW bug. It was orange, probably 1974. Luna and the bearded guy looked to be in love, or at least in some French-movie version of love. Driving together, they had recently quarreled, and now the fast-reversing shots of the guy (I think his name was Guy), and close-ups of Luna's thighs—crossed up high, on the passenger side, under a blue '70s miniskirt—led me to believe a reconciliation was imminent. No, it was obligatory, leading to the money shot. A slow pan of Luna's bare back, slender shoulders, and small breasts as she turned (a kind of lovemaking, French-style) let me know it was.

I closed my eyes and thought up a sexual position; opened my eyes to see if Luna and Guy were thinking the same. They would be, or they wouldn't, but it never mattered. I was lost now, completely in tune with the director's vision of the senses. I'd become the third party in Luna's love affair: the other man, a discreet voyeur. Necessary viewer. Not entirely masturbatory. I felt as though I were dreaming up these images. Pulse, beating. Brain, transforming.

My body slipped down in my seat until I was closer to the floor, more sprawled, than I was to sitting up straight. I finished the film in my head—going on with the dialogue and soundtrack still in my ears, still slightly aware—until the film ended and the classroom lights came on.

Students spilled out of the room and sent a buzz into the air. With the credits rolling, a few sighing heads stepping over my wounded boot that blocked the aisle, I was disaffected, as usual, and as usual, unaffected by what the class had offered me. Luna was dead now, in a fade out; faded. I couldn't push myself to go to my next class. I'd wait for the room to empty out completely to resume sleep.

But the cleaning lights came on—the ones that hang a kind of florescent haze over everything underneath them; over me in that auditorium, and behind my eyes, and inside my head. I peeked over the seats in front of me towards the now stark white and blank screen. A very tiny, very deliberate, ancient janitor wheeled in a bucket and mop. Hunched, bent at the waist, he wasted no time and worked quickly to slop water on the floor.

The old man slapped the mop inside the bucket; pulled it out, wrung out the dirty water, and slapped it back onto the floor with a wet smack. Probably humming a playful tune, the man with his mop and bucket were a single form. The way his arms moved the mop. The way the mop sucked back the bucket's water, the floor's filth. He covered a large area in good time with wide sweeps. But he was a blur: a human insect, a praying mantis wearing a janitor's uniform. Sweat stains under his armpits. The mop's long handle moved from side to side, long strings flapping. He was marking his environment with a kind of insect resin.

Once again, I wanted to become fully involved in what I saw, however I saw it. Maybe, I, too, was some kind of enormous bug. Cool, calm, coy. My bug eyes watching. Yes, we were two enormous cockroaches or freaked out insects, alive inside that one-time auditorium, now empty classroom.

I studied his movements, hypnotized by the rhythm of the mopping. The sounds echoed inside the big room, inside my head until watching no longer satisfied. I approached. Walked down the steps that led to the front, moving as a young bug might without fully formed wings, in a kind of larva stage.

The man shot his eyes at me, slightly startled. He noticed me for the first time. I liked the advantage. I could see things from all angles, shoot the scene my way. I stood against a wall and continued to watch.

The mopping slowed down, and the plunges into the slop bucket picked up. He peered up over his lost concentration to look at me. The frazzled little bug worked as best he could, until—possibly feeling a final threat, or a need to speak—he set down his mop and walked over. That's when I tried to leave.

His words were as stained as his blue shirt: he spoke in a thick Eastern European accent. He reached inside his pockets for a prop: his fat wallet. Inside, pictures of his grandchildren. Many. All ages. And the one, the old cockroach thought, reminded him of me.

I wanted out. Wished I'd never attempted the stalk in the first place. It had backfired into a friendly chat with a friendless old man. A non-bug, as it turned out. I was the only insect now, and felt my body contorting in the thick, segmented carapace. It was shedding a skin. My skull was dome-shaped. Antennae grew. Eyes bulged and pushed out from the sides of my big head. I fussed with the collar of my shirt. Ran fingers fidgeting through my buzzing hair. Nodded impatiently, mechanically. But the man wouldn't stop his rant.

I broke free. Let out a gasp—the breath, like a note I'd been holding—and kicked desperately at the water bucket. The fucking janitor jumped and fell backwards, pictures flying. The bucket tipped over. The mop fell to the ground. Water poured out and splashed up my pants. I bolted out of the room as the little man, bewildered, scrambled to collect the now wet photos and put them back in his bulging wallet. He stood as best he could and re-orientated himself, and himself to his ruined work.

Goodbye Grace

The pain was in my mouth, on the back part of my fat tongue. I stuck my index and middle fingers down my throat to find scales forming on the tissue. Reaching far inside the mucus to feel the size of the blisters, I started to gag and spit. I could taste bubbles of blood and bile, and

I had to pull out. There was darkness inside my body. Under the skin: sinews, muscles, fat, bone. I imagined shining, red rays beaming out, like projection lights, where they could from the holes: mouth, eyes, ears, asshole. Trapped inside my head and down inside my bowels, I exhaled a dense cloud of grey smoke through wide, flaring nostrils that seemed to spell out a foreign word in the frost-creased air: Merde.

Grace worked part-time at a café on the University of Toronto campus. I didn't remember the reasons for our last fight, but I was sure that it had blown over. That we'd made up, blowing each other. I'm sorry, I said, I'm sorry, you were right, I'm sorry...I don't know what gets into me...it's the light forcing its way out...no, you're right, it was my fault...

I finished my cigarette, sitting on the steps to the café. It had rained earlier and the steps were wet, making the seat of my pants wet.

Inside, the walls were yellow and the chairs and tables painted up in a starburst of orange and red. Grace wore her blonde hair up. Wore a uniform apron and comfortable blue jeans that made her ass and slim hips look small and cute. She was laughing behind the counter with a tall and skinny coworker, Allen. He was blowing hard about what had just happened to the coffee. They worked together at fixing an espresso machine that had exploded, leaving coffee grinds and foam all over the counter, on the floor at their feet, and on their aprons too. I passed by them, unnoticed. Went to the washroom in the back, pissed, and came back to their dark laughter. Grace was surprised to see me and immediately left her work behind the counter.

She pressed herself against my body and pecked me on the cheek with her red, bee-sting lips. She had deposited a little of the contents from the broken machine on my pants. The smell of the coffee made me gag. Or was it Grace? I dropped into a seat as she told the delightful story of Allen and the espresso machine.

I stared at the milk dripping off the counter. Started counting the drips, looking for a sequence in the drops. Tried to hear the milk hit the floor, blocking out all other noises, including Grace. Had I really known the girl a year? And what really did I know about her?

She was a fourth year student, studying the environment and urban planning. Yes, she was convinced that there was a way to salvage what remained of the ruined earth, and the chaos of the city. Her psycho-geography included saving the place from its broken-heart. Yes, her belief in what she called the good nature of things was what had first attracted her to me. A kind of innocence you see in silent films. Determined optimism. Everything had a place. She believed in order and was hearing the call. I had become her most recent and demanding urban project.

As she spoke, I could see a kind of admiration turned longing on Allen's face. Giggling on cue, nodding in recognition of the mishap, every cell was tuned in to what Grace had to say, and how she was saying it. He was staring at her mouth. I was staring at him. I checked for feelings of jealousy, or even disgust, but found none. I tried working myself up to a fever pitch, thinking about Allen at home in his pimpled bed, getting off on images of Grace, or how Allen's apron must really bulge when she brushes up against him behind that tight counter. But I felt nothing. And it wasn't that I couldn't imagine Grace with her arms and legs wrapped around this Allen. I could. I had. It was that I just didn't seem to care now.

Grace brought me a cup of black coffee. She could see that I wanted to sleep. The drink was hot and further numbed my tongue. It slithered down my throat and splashed around a bit before falling down inside my body.

I turned my head slowly towards the door as it opened. A couple entered, shaking rain off—the way dogs do—as they searched a menu board above an attentive Allen. Grace set to work with a dishrag on the tabletops. There was no doubt the place was a cafe, serving up coffee, tea, sugar, cream, desserts, juice, cakes, muffins, cinnamon rolls, biscuits, and sandwiches.

I stared blankly at Allen. Held my cup of coffee with both hands and began to blow. My lips were a pursed "O", and I moved my head clockwise, then counter-clockwise steadily. Allen did his best to ignore me as he waited on the indecisive couple.

Grace was to my right. Bent at the waist, she was cleaning off a round table, her body thrusting forward and back, her arm circling the top. It was a kind of dance I'd seen other waitresses do. Eyes glued to Allen, I continued the blowing act and moved my right hand towards her body. Allen looked away. I rested my hand on her back, quite affectionately as far as Grace could tell, and she glanced back and touched my arm

I caressed her, mirroring her arm movement on the table. Allen fought to keep his head down. I started to whistle. The sound was too alluring. When Allen caught back up with me, I slithered my hand down Grace's spine to her ass and thrust it between her thighs.

She jolted up from the goosing. Allen was fully terrified and demanded what kind of lattes his customers wanted with a cracking plea. Grace played a kind of indignant flirt and slapped me, scolding me in a whisper. I was disgusted at how far I was prepared to go, or to see them go.

Grace, a little turned on by the danger of it all, began to whistle herself and turned to another table, this time to the left of me. Staring at Allen with my mouth open, I flicked my insect tongue in and out and fluttered my eyelashes. I was in spasm, panting. I clawed at Grace. She reeled around, no longer playful. Annoyed. Not impressed. She glared at me.

Now, it would have been something if Allen had walked over to the table and challenged me to a fistfight, shirtless out back in the pouring rain. It would have been something if Grace had grabbed the scalding cup of black and thrown it into my face. It would have been something else if Grace had stripped naked on the spot and given herself over to an improvised lovemaking session for the needy watchers. But Allen turned his back on us and poured the drinks. The couple in the line of vision sat down and dried off. And Grace gave me a shoulder colder than her look.

The Assignment

It was a simple assignment. The camera was to remain stationary and, without the aid of dialogue or sound, we had to show an action: a single, still shot of thirty seconds. Everyone was excited because it was the first time that we would be shooting on real film. Everyone except for Bosco, who had money and had already shot a half-hour independent documentary on a hidden obsession of his—firemen and firefighting.

I balanced myself on a two-foot stepladder and fastened one of Bosco's large lamps to a tree. The others—Julie, Matt, Jen, and Lee—were busy complimenting Bosco on his choice of location (his parents' backyard in Rosedale) and Bosco's parents for their recent landscaping work.

Julie was made up for the shoot. She had a lovely face and a way about her. She'd at least bring something edgy to the film—a young, beautiful face onscreen to gawk at. But I was glad that she was not going to speak. She was to walk into the frame after a deliberate ten seconds of nothing and gesture off-camera. Bosco's pet hound, Vincent, was then going to run in with a stick in his mouth. Julie bends down, takes the stick, and rewards the animal. A simple creation dreamed up behind the heavy, dark eyelids of A. Bosco Rowens, Jr.

I set a standard three-point lighting, and relaxed into a lawn chair away from the group. My only interest in the project was the anticipation that when Julie bent down to give a dog a bone, I'd sneak a peek up her skirt. Pathetic, but true. I closed my eyes patiently.

Vincent was a real asshole of a dog. He was purebred, but mangy, and not in a good way as with dogs you want to rescue. He ran wild in the backyard, obviously overjoyed at the turnout for our shoot. He charged over to me and started sniffing in all the right places. The group laughed. Vince jumped up onto my lap and tried to lick my eyes. But a dog had already licked me that day, and I knew what always happens when you let them lick you. I hated Bosco, and I really hated his fucking dog. I shoved the dog off me and ignored the comments of the crew.

The first five takes were lost on the idiot mind of Vince, and the next three on Bosco. When I suggested that we just shoot Vince taking a shit, it was rejected. I suggested shooting Julie doing the same, then sneaking behind a bush. But we tried again with other ideas and got somewhat of a shot. Fin.

All hell broke loose sometime after that with Vince, the beast at the gates, and what I did to him. I was smoking now, alone in the back. I'd finished packing up the equipment and didn't join the others inside for celebratory spiked lemonade, even though I wanted to get the bad taste out of my mouth. But knowing that lemonade wasn't going to do it, I played the loner until Vincent decided to join me.

Hopped up on Julie's repeated treats—being the only to have snuck a peek—exacting some kind of revenge or other dog-scheme because his master was really cruel when no one was looking, and played the peanut butter on the pecker trick once too often, and in any case in need of being fixed, the dog went for me. Grabbed onto my already swollen, already dog-bitten leg, and gnawed away at it like a son-of-a-bitch. I tried kicking him off, but he held on and clamped his jaw down. I reflected on the excruciating pain for a moment. Felt it spread through my body. Felt something wild. I wanted to remember this sensation. The pain mounted. I managed to bend down and, with my still-burning cigarette, butted it out, deep and sizzling, into Vince's engorged doggy testes.

The poor beast yelped. I let go. Horrified. If only the camera could have been rolling for thirty seconds of that.

The Condemned Room

Next to the campus, the Park Hyatt Hotel tempted us students
with how its rooms started at $305 a night. With how there was a
luxurious spa in the entrance. Walking by, one could see the privileged
in privileged cucumber masks being massaged in spite of the fact that
their muscles only ached from being wealthy and high up in society.
There was a cigar and gift shop beside the spa, and that's where the
kids sometimes shopped at Christmas when they wanted to dance
with the elite and send presents back home that showed what kind of
life they were seeking out in the city: at university with the promise
of becoming a professional. I had fallen into the job my first year at
school and was glad that it offered me the opportunity to observe
people. But more and more, those people had turned me off so much
so that I was aching to quit.

I hobbled down a back alley to the employee entrance and
forced myself inside. From out of my locker, I disentangled a wrinkled
uniform tuxedo shirt, shook it out in front of me in the air and up over
my head. Let it fall like a parachute. The red bow tie was snug as a
noose. Jerry met me in the lobby and told me to attend to a special
guest checking in at the desk. (All the dirty, old bellhops knew all
the women who were staying with us.) Ms. Dorvier had three kids
with her. Their faces were lifeless masks. The youngest boy kicked at
his suitcase, bored. Dorvier ran her fingers through the boy's golden
hair as she signed off on a credit card receipt. The whole family was
gold-encrusted. Even the snot on the little boy's nose was deep ochre.
Jerry smiled and gave me his secret salute: his right hand formed a
fist and thrust three times to the tune of a syncopated whistle. The
old bastard wanted to watch her undress. I wheeled over a dolly and
gathered her luggage.

The Dorvier daughter scowled as we stepped inside the elevator.
Jerry turned and faced the children. I had seen this act countless times
before and refused to watch it again. Instead, I focused on Dorvier's
perfume—a mixture of hyacinth and brandy. Jerry displayed two
open hands for the children and, with a swift lift and tuck, produced
a fake flower from his left sleeve. The children weren't pleased by the
green-haired, amateur lizard-magician, despite the encouragement of
their beautiful mother. Jerry turned his back, stuffed the flower up
his arm, and faced the door. I looked down at the youngest boy with
the gold curls and glowing snot. Dorvier met my eyes then for the first
time. Her perfume seemed to drift more towards cognac. Stepping out

of the elevator to the seventeenth floor, I ran my fingers through her son's hair just to feel the locks of gold for myself.

A few hours into my shift, I was hiding on the thirteenth floor inside suite number three. The condemned room was unoccupied because of a malfunctioning heater. The place was like a sauna all year round. I knew Lucia, the chambermaid, wouldn't be coming in to clean the way she did that night the two of us discovered the cave and made love against the sweating oak chesterfield. I lit a cigarette and soaked my bloated ankle in the toilet. I stared out at the décor. The tapestries were deep, blood red with gold embroidery. The small dining room chandelier made a kaleidoscope patchwork on the hardwood floor. The smell of the over-bleached sheets made me nauseous. I swallowed hard to keep from puking all over the marble tiles. I mopped up the sweat from my temples with my sleeve and cleared the film from my eyes. I butted out my cigarette in the granite soap dish and flushed the toilet. I propped myself up on the lip of the bathtub and stepped back carefully inside my boots.

I managed to lie low for the rest of the night because the hotel was vibrating with action. Everywhere, all the arseholes were preparing for the opening night of the Toronto International Film Festival at the end of the week. Once again I was loathing myself, laughing at my one-time dream. As I watched how stupid people became at the nearness of other people's money and power, I decided that I, too, was a bullshit artist. Takes an asshole to know one.

As It Happens

Back at my apartment, I found my keys inside a mess deep inside my pocket, where I had stashed twelve dollars in tips broken down into coins, bits of paper, receipts, two different lighters, and cigarettes with exploding pieces of tobacco. The key out and in the door, it opened and the smell of marijuana hit me at the same time as the sound of Miles Davis and voices. Charlie sat smoking shirtless on my bed, and a girl with short, cropped black hair formed a perfect serpentine shape beside him. Charlie introduced me to a mildly high Roxanne, and told me that they had found the tap in the kitchen running when they showed themselves in earlier. Charlie had already set up my video camera on a tripod in the corner. He was trying to be a modern-day Andy Warhol, shooting life as it happens. He even wore large, black-rimmed glasses that he'd found in a vintage shop on Queen West, despite his perfect eyesight. He was also desperate to get

his hair all white like Warhol's. He had bleached it so many times that
his hairline showed signs of severe burns. I secretly wished that he'd
go bald, but then he'd just adopt a kinship to Jackson Pollock. He was
a bullshit artist's bullshit artist, but worse because he would never
admit it. I put up with him because I still clung to some half-cocked
notion of collaborating with him on films. The only things we shared,
up until that night, were stale breath and angst.

The talker turned off the piercing horn wailing in my room.
Charlie bombarded me with questions about Grace. He told me that
he was glad she was gone. Roxy slapped me hard, high up on the thigh
and told me to forget her, to move on.

The camera in the corner was taping over my bootlegged copy
of Touch of Evil that I'd filmed one noir night at the Bloor Cinema.
Charlie was hungry and out of Zig-Zag paper. He took ice cream
orders, dressed himself in my checkerboard housecoat and military
beret, and headed out the door. With Andy Arsehole gone, Roxy told
me that it had been bothering her all night, and she grasped around
at the clasp of her bra, undid it, removed it; a magic act underneath
her tight black t-shirt with a print of Che Guevera on it. Then she
began to play with the laces of my boots and managed to say through
slurred words that it was bad manners to keep shoes on in the house.
Pressed for time, and by Charlie's return, Roxy tried to untie my laces.
I flinched as she pushed down on my raw ankle. She caught me sitting
up, and we began to grab each other. Barely making contact, missing
every kiss, ripping at each other's clothes. I lay on my back, my face
pressed against her stretched rib cage. She had one hand inside my
pants, and moved her free hand down towards my boots.

An electric shock blinded me when she reached my wounded
ankle that sent a charged wave through my body. Roxy pulled up
my pant leg to reveal the gash. I saw it in that smoke-filled room,
like a third mouth, wet and throbbing. Roxy saw it like a mouth too
because she flicked at it with her warm, skinny tongue. She dragged
her bottom lip away, and we resumed as the camera watched us. Roxy
passed out soon after. I managed to put her bra back on, her shirt
back on. I pulled Che over her head. I wanted her to disappear, to
evaporate. I didn't want her there. I hadn't asked to know her and
resented everything about our new entanglement.

It had been half an hour, and I soon realized that this was
another of Charlie's bohemian schemes. It was another test. I'd failed.
But I decided to play along and not destroy the tape he'd so hoped

would catch a carnal betrayal. I capitulated not because of intrigue,
but indifference. I just didn't care. I figured my ass in the air would be
a fitting end to our friendship.

Tapes I'd Recently Made of Penelope
With Roxy asleep beside me, I turned on the television and popped
in one of the tapes I'd recently made of Penelope. She came alive, as
always, on the screen in front of me.

Penelope hangs a browned, bloodstained sheet with large,
wooden clothespins on a TV antenna. Her knuckles are red from the
fight; her work is blown reckless against the wind. Vines that frow in
twists on the brick wall shoot straight through the latticework of her
enclosed balcony.

The shot was ruined when I'd lost my balance leaning over a
railing of the adjacent building. My frenzied camerawork showed
the near fifty-foot drop. I remember reaching over and grasping the
machine as if it were a falling body. The frame went to black as I
secured it in a bag under my arm. I remember shimmying out onto a
ledge, bracing myself for the jump, refusing to look down, and leaping
across, making it safely to her terrace. Then the video reopened on the
screen-less window of her apartment, but still my eyes couldn't focus
as I peered inside her place.

Penelope is expressionless on the edge of her bed as she dips a
cloth into a basin and brings it to an old woman's face. The face is
gaunt and grimacing. It peers out from a mess of blankets like a mask.
Water trickles down her forehead and into stone eyes that open from
the invasion. She bats Penelope's hand away and sits up, knocking the
basin to the floor. A fat, orange cat reels out from under the covers and
begins to investigate the new puddle. Penelope tends to the mess as the
old woman starts a coughing fit—falls back onto a flat yellow pillow
and tries to breathe. The orange cat plays in the water, and Penelope
exits the room. The woman sticks her hand between the mattress and
box spring and retrieves a book of matches and a pack of cigarettes.
She strikes a match with unsteady hands, and lets out a string of
curses when the spark refuses to become flame. Penelope re-enters
the room and wrestles the smokes away from the woman. The fight
is effortless and one-sided. Penelope moves towards the window and
pitches the woman's contraband outside. It lands by my trembling
foot. The old woman kicks at the television screen, buzzing snow at
the foot of her bed. Penelope turns off the set and brings in a black

kimono, detailed with a gold dragon and purple orchids on the back. The old woman climbs out of bed and into the robe. Penelope escorts her by the arm and leads her into the bathroom. The shot is through the fogged-up, far left window, reflected in a mirror above a sink.

Penelope strips the woman and helps her into a large claw-foot tub. The woman gasps, shrieks, because the water is either too hot or too cold. Penelope supports the woman's quivering head with a brown sponge. The room is quiet except for a dripping faucet and a buzzing, florescent bulb. Penelope helps the woman out of the tub. Water runs down her naked, emaciated body. Penelope dries her with a large, white towel. They return to the other room. The woman sits hunched in a high-backed wicker chair facing a mirror. Penelope combs the woman's tangled mass of black hair with a star-shaped comb. She begins to cut into the curls. The sound of the scissors is coarse, like sandpaper against stone. The woman's bangs are left crooked and blunt, a kind of asylum fringe.

The screen went black. My battery had died. The final few shots were sabotaged by the suspicions of the orange cat meowing and scratching at the sash.

I looked over to Roxy asleep in my bed. She was snoring. She seemed so much smaller than she had when she was awake, as if being unconscious had deflated her. I was scared to look at her, let alone touch her again.

Pools of Crystal
Knowing her routine in the night, I took a cab to Regent Park. On cue, Penelope emerged from her building dressed in a bright yellow raincoat. Under the low light of the street lamp, unfiltered, her skin was less translucent. She carried a canvas bag over her shoulder that swung violently in time with her walk. I steadied my camera.

I didn't go inside the liquor store immediately. I waited back a few moments before crossing the street. Inside, I lost sight of her and struggled to search over a display tower of sambuca bottles. I hid my camera in my coat. I moved too quickly, catching a glimpse, and bumped into the four-tiered setup. Glass crashed as the bottles teetered and fell to the ground. All eyes were on me. The black liquorice liquor seeped through my boots. A stock boy who looked as if he had a fake left ivory eye advanced toward the mess and gave me an awful sideways glance, a cyclops stare. I swear I could see Penelope in its fractured reflection.

She was clutching a bottle of solera rum in her arms. She seemed unmoved by my collision and paid no attention. I bent down to see what I could salvage. The syrupy sambuca and the shattered glass sparkled on the floor like a drowned chandelier. Reaching inside the pool of crystals, I ripped my palm open. The stock boy told me to move on. I left a trail of blood as I made my way out the door.

I was sucking on my wounded hand in the alley behind the liquor store. I spit out a tiny shard of glass. A large metal door sprung open, and I went scurrying behind a dumpster. The skin on the back of my neck: goose-pimpled. The store manager was stuffed inside a puke-blue shirt and tie. His face hung off him like hot wax. His red, swollen hands were blistered, clutching Penelope's wrist. They looked like lobster claws in the dim light of the alley. The moon seemed to wink, solar-eclipsed, and I didn't know if I'd be able to make the shot in the rain. But I pulled out and palmed my camera anyway. Penelope floated out onto the concrete, being dragged. Her canvas bag was stuffed with bottles of rum that jostled together and resounded like bells in a burnt-down cathedral. She was soft as nails, and refused to look the manager in his fat face. She collapsed to her knees, wilted like a flower after a storm, and set to work on the throbbing, bloated monster; paying for her stolen rum. His pleasure was uttered in moans and quivering gasps. I refused to focus the frame on the hands that held Penelope's hair. Instead, I spotted an engorged rat trapped inside a hole in the building's brickwork, and tried to steady my hand enough to film its attempt to burrow inside the wall.

Penelope's silhouette was made of origami rice paper. She lay crumpled on the ground now, as the manager staggered back inside. I zoomed in on her retrieving a bottle of rum from her bag, guzzling, spitting out a spray of the makeshift mouthwash. A fine mist lingered in the air. When she seemed satisfied with the taste on her tongue, she swallowed and remained motionless. She closed her eyes as if in surrender or sleep. I was held hostage by the subtlety of her breathing. Every minute I left her that way, alone on the ground, she became more and more rain-soaked.

From somewhere sudden inside her—her belly, or the pit in her chest—a reverberation began to echo out, violent and jagged. Penelope was laughing like a belching sinkhole. Horrified laughter. I couldn't bear the sound. I wanted to run. Desire had been replaced by fear. Overwhelmed now by the shrieking woman and the rain, I shoved my camera inside my bag and took off running. Badly hobbled

by my limp, I tripped and fell face-first onto the sprawled girl. Her fit
was silenced by the surprise. We were both frantic to orient ourselves.
I tried to stand up. Penelope pushed me away from her. The struggle
was awkward though savage. Penelope got to her feet first and pulled
out a small black can of mace and unloaded the poison squarely into
my face. My eyeballs burned, and tears streamed down my cheeks.
I pressed my forehead against the concrete, but the coolness of the
stone wouldn't soothe me.

     Black came over me slowly, although I was frantic, rubbing my
eyes with clenched fists. The light seemed to ooze out of my grasp. I
felt sick to my stomach, as if I'd sucked on battery acid, or eaten a
piece of raw ground beef. Penelope resumed her laughing, and started
to pour rum down my back. I was powerless as she tried to snatch
away my bag and reached into my pants for my wallet. From the
sound of her throat, I thought she was standing over me. I reached
out in protest and suddenly understood the depth of my blindness. I
could feel her poking at me from different angles, toying with me as
if I were a wired toy mouse. She moved around me and through me
until she'd had enough and finished me off with a vicious kick to the
balls. I vomited instantly. It was as if a tree was growing roots in my
groin and branches were rising up through the veins in my abdomen,
pushing through my shoulders and armpits. The last thing I heard
before passing out was her calling me motherfucker and running off.

Delirium

I saw my film clearly as I lay blind in the alley. My brain exploded in
images once I accepted the pain, or so I thought. I was grateful for
it, for visions beyond my own boredom and self-loathing, beyond my
contended, spoiled, smug situation at school. I had never longed to
create as intensely as I did at that moment. Never had I wanted to
connect with another person or thing as badly as I did while sprawled
out in the gutter.

     My eyes rolled back in my head: a flashback for my film—
Penelope's youth. Running away from home—the home, a farmhouse,
a kind of madhouse itself—possessed, it seemed, by the spirit of
reckless abandon, and a family growing wild, like weeds, and the
animals dying and the field going to seed. And her mother's childhood
was a field of ashes too, because she never did make it to her father's
funeral, and the old man was a beautiful, albeit nasty and abusive,
drunk—just like she is—and it's too bad they didn't have the money

to bury him under his favorite oak. And the portrait she painted of her first husband comes to life because she always loved painting, and that's the only one she didn't burn. Besides, he was a noble man when all was said and done. And surely this made up for the fact that he bored her at times. And now she added something new to the old painting, knowing more now than when she painted it on her honeymoon. His heart raked with sores. The sort of thing only a wife can paint when she runs off and leaves her high school sweetheart to turn sour. She hops on a subway. The tunnel is truly endless because she hasn't realized that she's left a six-year-old Penelope back at the last stop. And all the passengers are patients she's met in shelters, in madhouses, in hospitals and motels. And they all shake their heads and judge, as if they know better. And Penelope's mother smashes the windows with bare fists to try to get out, but the fists turn into heads of kittens that she's had and had taken away from her because poverty is the only thing that doesn't change when you sleep.

There was a dream in it and a film in it. But really, I knew nothing of Penelope Moon, or her mother. I lacked the kind of discipline that makes the unseen visible to the naked eye, and I lacked empathy. Unable to shoot life as it happens because I could not give up my desire to control what I shot. There could never be any honesty because I was a hack, manipulating everything around me as if it were my own.

Renunciation

My eyes still on fire from the mace, I walked home, out of focus. Toronto was burning. Every night crawler seemed smudged against the concrete landscape. When I got back to my apartment, Roxy was still asleep. Looking around, I took note for what felt like the first time of my burned out place. I saw everything differently now, as if Penelope Moon had cast a strange, brilliant light throughout. The ray shone on my desk, littered with papers and unfinished script ideas, and on a kitchen mess that was happy just to soak in water at the bottom of the sink. The light made strange shadows: made my bookshelf seem bigger than it was, and my stereo, smaller. I didn't recognize the faces in photos on the wall because their features were filmy and unfamiliar. Had she brought all this? She had, because I no longer wanted anything to do with my room, unless it had her in it. I wanted no part in school, unless she was there.

Goodbye, tuxedo uniform, wrinkled mess by my feet. Goodbye,

friends. I overturned photos in frames. Goodbye, school. I grabbed
a stack of papers, grabbed unpaid phone bills, even grabbed the
phone. I was clearing it all away. I wanted to be stripped down. My
DVD collection and my Marlene Dietrich poster, and the answering
machine, and my bicycle with the flat tire, and my music collection,
bedspread, and rug, I heaved everything out onto the balcony. A mess
from a messed up life that was no use to me: discarding it had been
a long time coming. The noise eventually woke Roxy, who looked at
me through smoke-filled eyes. I had forgotten her name and didn't
know what to call her. She was clearly startled by my freak show. And,
freaked out, she got up quickly, and left.

All that remained was my TV, VCR, my camera, and the
Penelope tapes. I couldn't let them go. I was out of breath and weak,
but my vision was coming back, despite the burning. I turned on the
set and replayed the tape I'd made of Penelope and her mother—the
Moon women. It played to the end. I rewound it and watched it again,
and again. I was grasping at a way of understanding that seeing them
was enough.

I heard pounding at the door—the super surely wanted to talk
about the disturbance. I hoped that it was the super so I could take
the eviction with the same conviction I would begin the new phase,
if that's what this was. I unlocked the deadbolt and opened the door.
Some huge, longhaired guy in a goon suit pushed his way in. Behind
him trailed Penelope Moon and her mother.

Awake
After emptying my fridge of a few beers and the last pack of pepperoni
sticks, the goon asked for payment. I didn't know for what, and I had
nothing, so he took my camera and slapped me across the face. Then
he tossed a bag of pills at Penelope and left.

The Moon women were different in person. I thought I knew
their faces and bodies well from all the camera angles, but in my room,
in real life and in real time, they terrified me. Penelope told me she
got my address from my wallet. I couldn't imagine what they wanted
from me. I had nothing.

Penelope dished out a handful of pills to her mother, and
swallowed one herself. Her mother climbed into my bed and instantly
fell asleep. Penelope told me to put on a video that I'd made of her.
She wasn't angry. Or, if she was, she didn't say. I tried to explain
myself, but she shushed me and pointed to her sleeping mother. I put

on one of the videotapes. Penelope told me to go and get something to eat and to be back before her mother woke up. I obeyed.

On the street again, I felt more awake than I had for a long time. Not well rested—because I was exhausted—but sober, alert, and awake. How many times had I been asleep or pretended to be while others called or came looking for me? While the world and its jumbled mess kept turning in circles, and while I was so tumbling, drowsy, or unconscious, I had stayed safely hidden inside my head.

Maybe it was because I had accepted the fact that my camera was gone, or that my apartment had been taken over by the Moon women, or that I was beat on and bruised and ripped through and burning, and could still barely see—whatever the reasons, I started to cry like a baby. I bawled my eyes out as I walked through the pitch-black campus. Licking my tears as they rolled down to my mouth, they, bitterly enough, tasted sweet. I felt that if I could just drink up enough sweet tears, I'd at least be left with a fine taste in my mouth. So I concentrated on crying. Weeping. For myself and my chewed-up ankle and the nightmares that Vince the dog was having, and for Grace and for the old janitor I'd stalked and abandoned. For the woman who had sprayed me with mace and had shut out the visible world for a while. I was putting names and needs to every face that I'd ever ignored.

All the lights on Bloor Street were stretching and being blown by the way I saw them through eyes that were bleeding tears. Everything was a shooting star, was a strobe light, was a ray projected from a movie house, was a firestorm. The only light that stayed its true blue colour was the pale, gray-blue moon. That moon, a scrim in the sky, appeared above me like a stark white cinema screen.

It was only Professor Wylie passing by on his retro brown bicycle with a basket of books and videos that sobered me up.

I was startled to hear my name and startled that I had a name and was still a human being. I wiped frantically at my face and eyes and got a few more licks in, but the sweetness wasn't doing anything for me now. Wylie leaned back on his high school counselling days and didn't push, only remarked on the night and almost the moon, too, and the times we both found ourselves living in. Sure, he felt sad, too, outraged that over in the Middle East there was yet another suicide bombing, that afternoon. He wasn't going to cry, but certainly didn't mind that I was letting the tears fall. He hadn't cried since 1980, the day John Lennon was shot. Imagine being twenty-three then, Len.

And some things never change; and don't get sad, get active. He gave me a flyer for an anti-war march taking place after Thursday's class and a brief introduction to 'Outsider Cinema,' and he chimed off to attend an all-night film event.

I tried adding the death of John Lennon to my list of tears and those victims in the Jerusalem bombing too, despite the fact that I didn't even know where the war was being fought these days.

I stopped in at the McDonald's across from the museum and grabbed a bunch of crap to feed Penelope and her mother.

Dark Laughter

The inside of my room was desolate and cold—a slate-blue ruin. I felt as though I was walking on the surface of the moon. The eerie silence was disturbed only by the cradlesong of Penelope's mother who rattled away with pebbles in her throat.

Penelope told me that her mother had been dying for forty years. The girl couldn't concentrate. She ate her French fries with loud smacks and slurped savagely at her vanilla milkshake. She wanted to see more footage. More evidence against me.

I put on a tape from outside of the mission where the two women would eat on Friday nights. I had never been able to work up enough courage to set foot inside the church basement; it had all been shot from safely across the street. The lineup was torn and disjointed: a hungry ruckus. Penelope scanned the screen and said she couldn't find herself or her mother. I paused the footage to show her where they were, but Penelope said that she couldn't see a fucking thing. She grew bored, criticized my camera work as especially shaky. She was the one who called me a hack.

A chance capture from last winter outside the Centre for Addiction and Mental Health, but again, I was so well hidden inside the sandwich shop across the street that the few glimpses of Penelope on the screen were of little interest to her. She denied that she was on the tape. The less interest she showed, the more I panicked and began to doubt it all—every shot, every stolen angle of their lives.

The frail body in my bed woke up coughing. Penelope went to her mother and gave her some of the fast food that I'd brought. I heard hysterical laughter as I sat on the floor outside my room. They were talking about me. Mocking me. I was a joke to them, tucked away inside my artsy shit-ass studio apartment. All I could offer was a Big Mac and large fries.

Their laughter and lip smacking grew louder; I was irrelevant,
I could barely hold their interest. The moving images I had taken
of them dissolved with each note of dark laughter sounding in their
throats. My little apartment was now an asylum occupied by Moon
women. And so was my head.

I couldn't imagine shooting them now, even though they had
appeared in front of me like magic. I had dreamed them up and
manipulated them like mannequins, or so I thought. And now they
had been delivered to me, right into my very own film set, but I
couldn't move, couldn't set up the shots, couldn't even dream it.

Red Carpet Treatment

Stumbling out onto the street, the women arm-in-arm controlled
everything in their path. I floated behind them as if attached by a
piece of string. Penelope hailed a cab, and the three of us piled in. The
hotel was only a few blocks away from my apartment in the Annex,
but they demanded VIP treatment since we were going to mingle with
the stars.

The taxi pulled up behind a parade of limos. Blinding flashes of
paparazzi lit up those clamouring to catch glimpses of the Hollywood
elite. I was disgusted. The cameras were in spasm.

I pulled out my employee pass and led the women into the hotel,
well off the beaten path of the red carpet, and took the elevator to the
thirteenth floor—to the condemned room.

Louis Ciel

Voices and the hum of bodies moving around me were coming together.
A rising fog of noise, filling the air, was bearing down on me, making
it hard to see. Making my skin buzz, glazing over my eyes, and sealing
up the holes in my body. I couldn't concentrate on work. I leaned
against a back wall in one of the hotel's dining halls. The meeting
was a press conference, or a converging of some kind, for the men and
women in charge of this year's film festival.

The menu promised first-class cuisine, and the bar was all
fireworks, or Bloody Maries, or screwdrivers, or champagne. And
the red carpet was all A-list. I had even laid some of it down myself.
And though my coworkers were lost in stargazing gossip, the stars all
looked shorter in person to me. We made them famous. We needed
stars so we could look up to something, but they were indifferent to
us. We were bending over backwards to make others feel important

so we could feel important by gawking at them. I was watching the clock, and I'd never resented time as much as I did at that moment.

I looked up at huge hands of time—really the hands of an antique and bronze clock that hung above the doors to the hall—and they seemed more like arms than hands: two enormous, steady arms, embracing me, controlling me.

Of course, I held some glimmer of hope somewhere inside at the promise of meeting Louis Ciel. The legendary French filmmaker was one of many responsible for my love of film. I was indebted. Ciel was on the guest list, and his latest film, Pas Encore Mon Amour!, was premiering at the festival, but there was no sign of him yet.

I knew where to find the real stars of my epic. It was, of course, a daring move, smuggling them in, but my offering was a four-star deathbed for Penelope's mother. I was grasping at a way of meaning something to them. They were indifferent to me. I was at their mercy. And in this way, Penelope and her mother were on the guest list. They were resting peacefully on a queen-sized hotel bed, albeit dusty and sub-standard. And in this way, too, I offered myself as a kind of servant or exclusive butler to my beloved guests.

Another perfect storm of camera flashes, flashing and bursting in the hall, heralded the entrance of another star. The eyes on these strangers, the attention that was being paid to them, weighed me down. This was true make-believe. And someone at the podium, some master of ceremonies, was narrating this fairytale. I was entirely anonymous. A vision of angst-rebellion flashed its way into my head: I turned the light into thunderclaps, then into fire, and I imagined myself an arsonist, vigilante-style, blowing up the whole damn room. Clearing it all away with a cry of protest.

Maybe I'd kidnap Louis Ciel before starting the fire, grill the man on the hidden secrets of foreign film practice, like how the fuck do you get the light to be so brilliant in your films? But really, I already knew. It was from a sun that shone down on the land and faces and through the camera across the ocean. And to see that, to bask in that, I'd have to set out on some kind of mad pilgrimage, which, if it weren't for lack of money, I'd have already set out on. Europe? Africa? Anywhere but in that lower east dining hall.

Needing air, I skulked out into the back alley behind the hotel. I found a moment of relief away from the crush. A truck was parked close to a delivery door, its engine idling. The exhaust fumes mingled with my own as I lit a cigarette and puffed away. The driver—a red, round, overworked type, wearing square shorts that ran past his knees with a high-riding Mickey Mouse t-shirt—stepped out of his cab. He was tearing at his hair and wiping beads of sweat from his bloated face. He carried a clipboard with a collection of dog-eared papers. He was lost and asked me to keep watch of his load as he went in to the hotel.

I peered inside the truck to find stacks of film canisters. They were lifeless—dead film inside their metal armor. I reached into the truck, grabbed the first case I saw, and ran.

Get the Cat

I hid the film reels under the bed in the condemned room. Penelope and her mother were both asleep. I moved in and closed the creaking door behind me. Penelope opened her eyes—those two round green glass jewels—and looked at me as if still asleep. Or rather, still in her dream, only now awake and conscious, too. She sat up. Kneeling beside her, I kissed her lips. My recent theft had empowered me.

They loved it there. And they could even see their place from the window, so high up. I peered outside at the city, but how could you see the house from way up here? All I saw was a maze of shapes and colliding buildings. Clutter is something only the virtuous can sort out. But no, she could see her home, and remarked that she'd never seen this hotel from her window.

A kind of dread, or sudden realization, appeared and washed over her face then, as she zoomed in on what my eyes searched for: the house, or at least even the neighbourhood. The cat. Oh yes, Monk.

"We've left Monk, and he hates being alone."

And my exhaustion from what had been the monumental task of being close to the one I longed for would now see me smuggle in a third castaway. Penelope demanded that I go to her place and get Monk.

"And I'm sure he's fine. But if you won't go, then I will."

And Penelope's determination gave me a glimpse of how she got things done, how deliberate and knowing she could be, though seemingly lost. Perhaps, then, Penelope and her mother had, in fact, all the answers. Perhaps, yes, this was the only way to survive. And they knew all they needed to know about this thing called life: control it, or it controls you. After all, didn't they occupy a suite, if not only the entire searching soul of a young, almost visionary, but failed filmmaker?

So I would have to leave my hidden paradise on the thirteenth floor, where everything had been made new, everything enchanted. I assured Penelope that I'd find a way to bring back the cat before the night was through. And a simple smile, and here are the keys, showed that Penelope was confident in me and knew that I would obey.

Leonard in Wonderland

Without her around, haunting the place, I hated the street. It was empty, and my walk felt forced without that magnetic pull, not to mention the limp. I did find the house, in spite of it all, and took out the key she had given me even though the lock was broken and the door ajar.

How easy it had been, I thought, to enter someone's life. Only now, stumbling through half-lit rooms, looking for the cat, did I realize my presence in someone else's life. Here, no longer trespassing, no longer spying, but opening myself up for someone else to shine through me and inside me. Only now did I find myself somewhere. And if only there were someone, some witness peering inside the house, or on top of the neighbour's balcony now to see me there.

Trying to think up a way to sneak an animal into the hotel without anybody seeing me was part of my new life. But this was my first chance to get to know more about the Moon women. Monk watched as I opened up dresser drawers and looked through boxes in the closet. There was a huge wooden jewelry box that would speak volumes if I had only known the stories behind all the broken jewelry, those heirlooms and assorted pieces of abandoned history. The women had taken the essentials with them—their bodies, their wild ideas, their needs, and whatever clothes they felt suited the adventure. But shelves of wine glasses and old decorative glass antiques and an oak chest with moth-eaten dance costumes, photos of a young Helena Moon (at last a name for her mother) in the wilderness, and flowered quilts, and a broken rocking chair, and huge burnt-out lamps—this was the stuff of flea markets, of junkyards, and Salvation Army store storage rooms. It was all very appropriate for the ruined fairy kingdom, this gypsy dwelling. They were a couple of hoarders.

I was pillaging through the stuff, hoping to glimpse anything remotely familiar to me, to my own history. But as I searched for a link through discarded rum bottle after rum bottle, I just couldn't find one. And so it was Leonard in Wonderland, until the Cheshire cat rubbed and purred up against me and broke my trance.

Trapped Cat

The cat fit inside my jacket. If Monk would play sleeping cat clinging to my body, we'd have no problem getting into the hotel room. I'd just have to remain still and protect the huge bulge under my coat. But my allergy to cats was beginning to threaten our invasion. My poor eyes were gushing out something awful. It was all I could do to keep from scratching them out; I could barely keep back the tears. But I was working with patience and stealthy calm and remained driven. Besides, I quite liked the way Monk was purring against my body. I felt almost holy, carrying a living being, even though claws dug into my skin.

I went in and barely dodged a coworker, Randy, as he made his way to the elevators. Luck was on our side as it had been the night before, for truly, chaos was brimming inside the walls of the hotel. We were going unnoticed, because even though I was lumpy and snotty it was no scene amidst the real circus dressed up in chic blue suits and matching neckties.

On the elevator, I breathed easy and even stroked my belly, reassuring an indifferent Monk. But the pressure from the elevator's ascent jolted the cat, and he shimmied his way up to my chest, trying to orient his fat, furry self. I shoved the cat back down with a gentle but quick and firm hand, and zipped up my jacket all the way to my chin. The elevator stopped at the ninth floor. A couple got on and only noticed the oddity of the scene when the elevator's climb once again startled Monk. They watched as my gut contorted up to my collar, then back down again, while I faltered on a sneeze that became a laugh because the cat had inadvertently clawed at my crotch. I was being transformed in front of them. The elevator stopped again, and Monk and I made our getaway, though we had only reached the twelfth floor.

The commotion was enough to put Monk on alert, and he became what he truly was: a trapped cat inside a human bag, the bag running down the hall towards the stairs. I bounded past guests, got caught up by the opening and closing of room doors with the same urgency as Monk. We both longed for freedom. Both fought our confinement, regardless of the boundaries. This was the instinct of survival, and this need was the greatest until I was stopped frozen in my tracks as I turned a corner. Monk clawed and scrambled around inside me, and I stared into the eyes of the idol, Louis Ciel.

The French master was anything but shocked to see it: me,

panting, a statue about to explode from the inside out, while I stared into his Parisian blue eyes, as if I were watching every image the man had ever filmed. Every sunset, or moon dance, all the made-up lovemaking scenes and close-ups of French goddesses, and wide-angle crane shots of the Eiffel Tower in spring.

Monsieur Ciel showed no signs of knowing me. He left me to find the back stairwell and continue on up to the condemned room. Penelope Moon welcomed me, if only for the sake of the cat attached to my ripped-up body. He jumped out of my jacket and, free at last, ran over to Penelope who was on a couch watching TV, volume turned down, fully aware of her squatter's rights. Monk purred madly in her arms before leaving to investigate his new surroundings.

I slumped down beside Penelope and half-attempted to describe the adventure. But knowing that the whole matter was mine, and that she didn't really care, I stayed away from the inconvenience of it all and lay appeased in her lap, the fingers of her right hand running through my tangled hair, calming me.

The TV's reception was bad and played, through snow, Hitchcock's Rear Window. I couldn't help but be drawn in by it again. Penelope was happy to watch her cat paw the furniture and sniff the room, perhaps looking for her mother, Helena. If I had changed the channel to the news coverage of the Film Festival, that opening night ceremony taking place only floors below us, I would have seen her. Helena Moon, forever ready for some action, saying, "And why should I just stay here in the room to die?" She was dressed in a wild, saucy dress that all the actresses' stylists would agree on. She was mingling with and charming fellow guests. With a drink in one hand and a cigarette holder in the other, she was part of the scene. Perhaps a little too drunk, but she had class, if that's what you wanted. She knew how to dance and how to laugh. The string of pearls some lover had given her at one time was swinging majestically around her neck, and although almost gone, she wasn't yet dead.

Penelope eased my concern and told me her mother would be fine down at the party; and besides, there was no stopping her once she wanted something. And would it not be worse for me to go down and seek her out? Did I think I could capture this woman? Save her? Watch over her? Bring her back? She'd be half a mile high by now and flirting with the most important men there. She'd be making them curse God for ever taking this leading lady, this heroine, out so soon.

Exhausted, I lay still as Penelope tended to the cat scratches on

my chest. Cleaning them with a warm and wet cloth, then kissing my
body with warm and wet lips. I understood then, lying there still, that
the two Moon women would do as they pleased.

Femme Fatale

Helena is truly drifting, almost floating around down at the gala
event, her movements free and easy, the way they have to be in order
to keep up appearances. It's a kind of farewell ball, drawn up in her
honour. Now a frenzied tango plays, and some—uptight and trapped
inside their bodies, their expensive clothes, the room—fantasize, in
their wall-flowered state, that they can dance like her. And even if the
scene is one of horror—because steadily she is making her way closer
to death—it is not unlike any of her romantic plunges into the heart
of things.

    If we are dancing, let's dance. If we are drinking, drink up. If it's
death, and we're all dying, let's get it over with. Indeed, her hysteria is
a final and glorious exit—a lesson in how her heart is pumping madly
to keep up with her wild spirit. Her body is on display. Her sickness
laughs at the world. She's making love to the room, to the noise and
air and light in the room. And her skin shows itself to be rosy and
glowing, even though beneath, the paleness of the end is stark white
doom. A final turn of the ballroom finds a trickle of blood at the
corner of her gaping wound of a mouth. It drips down her chin and
dribbles on the dance floor. She's no longer keeping her disease all to
herself.

    A tall gentleman, disenchanted by the party and enchanted
only by her—a well-off director of some sort, impeccably dressed
and silver-haired—makes his way over to Helena just seconds before
she collapses out of her life-lived exhaustion, and into his arms. And
the rich, clean, French gentleman feels fire in her voodoo body. "Let
me help you, miss." And yes, he is the epitome of the tall, dark, and
handsome kind. "And what room are you staying in?" "And let me
take your drink." But Helena Moon manages to shoot back one last
gulp before he ushers her out. And why not—he sweeps her off her
feet into his strong arms towards the elevator, up to her room.

    Helena's breathing is soundless, though heavy, as her chest
heaves up and down with what are her last gasps of air. The man stares
at her, and he is transfixed, watching, unknowingly, the life surface on
her face and body. She has danced through, as in the ballroom, as the
downpour and assault leave their marks on her skin like pictures on a

screen. And though he tries to speak to her, to wake her, or even just stop her from laughing, he can only watch—the whole time wondering how he will ever retell this event in a film. And really, how accurate can he be? Knowing nothing but that he has this mad heroine dying in his arms, and that they are riding together in an elevator.

Proof

The door opened, and I peeled myself off of Penelope. Louis Ciel appeared before us carrying Penelope's mother in his arms. There was no strain in his face as he lay the woman down on the bed. Penelope was immediately at her mother's side and jumped into bed with her. I scrambled to find my clothes. They lay in a heap by the great filmmaker's feet. Monsieur Ciel pulled out a gold cigarette case and from inside it, a Gauloise cigarette, which he lit in a single gesture. I zipped up my pants and knelt beneath him as ashes fell on me. I wanted him to absolve me. But he snorted instead and pointed at me with his forefinger and thumb cocked like a pistol.

I couldn't join Penelope on the bed. The difference between her mother sleeping and her mother now, lying dead, was a subtle one. The true proof came in the woman's awkward tilt of the head. Her skin was still as pale blue as ever. I had never looked at a dead person before. She was weightless, blank. I understood a new depth of stillness as Penelope shook her like a rag doll.

Louis Ciel and I backed away from the scene. If he was as terrified as I was, he didn't show it. Yet we were both transfixed by the scene that played out before us. Transfixed, but useless, and we could only stare. Penelope was wrestling with the dead and losing. I was a slug, watching. My body was stuck, and I felt as though I would surely dissolve into the floor. I remained that way, a pair of dead eyes.

A team of paramedics pushed their way into the room. Louis Ciel began to explain the situation in accented English. My manager appeared out of nowhere and snapped me back to real life.

The Money

I sat in the hotel's back office, numb and deaf to the questions, indifferent to my dismissal. All the rules had been broken, and even if they would be pressing charges, what would it really mean? My only concern now was how Penelope would manage affairs at the hospital, and whether or not she would find a government funeral completely inappropriate for her mother, who for a long time had fought the system, which now held possession of her body. They would have no choice but to give her a pauper's grave, however unfit she deemed the burial.

In the end, it was money, always about money. It was either too much, or too little. You had to have enough to say fuck you to the charity of others. And now I sat only feet away from the office safe, where stacks of un-deposited envelopes of cash lay on top. I stared at the wads of monetary freedom. If I stole enough, I could leave right away. Penelope and I could escape the city. I'd have enough to finance a film.

So I was resolute. And when my boss presented his back in a passionate lecture about my breach of trust, I snatched up an overstuffed envelope and hid it inside my jacket pocket. My manager wheeled around at the noise to see a sudden flurry of emotion, my greatest performance. I threw myself onto his desk, sobbing and imploring through mad riffs of explanation, and why I wanted the two women there, and that one of them was dead now, and I was so confused.

And really, I was truthful in my performance, pure in my confession, except for the fact that I had that bulge of hundred dollar bills tight in my jacket.

So attached now to nothing but my own will, to obligations to myself and to my cooked-up plans, I walked out of that hotel and walked away from a discarded life. Armed with my stolen cash, I passed strangers in tuxedos who had disappointed me and whom I, too, had disappointed. Our failure was complete: it was in the film I dreamed.

The Spool

In the lobby, Louis Ciel was decked out in appropriate French garb, a blue silk scarf around his neck and a beret cocked atop his magnificent head. In his arms, that legendary filmmaker held Monk, the cat, who must have run away earlier and roamed through the halls looking for compassion. He was purring under Ciel's gentle hand. Answering the questions of a camera crew set up for his film's upcoming premiere, Ciel stroked the cat.

As I moved past the elegant entourage, Monk poked his head up over Ciel's adopted grandfather grip, and I accepted this gesture in the hopes that cats, like dogs, forgive the foolish acts of desperate men.

I was escorted from the hotel by two security guards, but no one was interested in watching the eviction. I was hustled out past the infestation of paparazzi and screaming fans. The mob swarmed like frenzied insects feeding on rot. I backed away into the night and stared up at the moon. The crowd also searched the sky, because from out of the window on the thirteenth floor, a crazy girl hung over the sill, screaming at the city. Her hysteria commanded the crowd and even the night as she held out a film canister as if it were a bomb. Then releasing the spool as though launching a kite, miles of footage spilled over the ledge and hurtled down towards the street below, where I was still dreaming of shooting Penelope Moon.

Film

In it, projected on the moon, I'm riding the narrow streets on a blue motorcycle. And I'm wearing a tight black t-shirt, the one I keep for fantasies like this. And Penelope is there, too, dressed in blue with my camera around her neck and her arms around me, dreaming up names for the films we're dreaming up. Her favourite: Rebirth. But I won't compromise for the sake of these hallucinations. I see her laughing less and less at those back home where we left them playing kiss-and-tell with the dead.

The camera pans the factories and fast food empires, cinemas and hotels and stars on the red carpet, and Penelope prays for them, even as she laughs at them in the dark. She blows them kisses: kisses for the sad ones, kisses for the numb, kisses for the unlucky, and even the lucky ones. She kisses an old man leaning on his mop. She kisses the junkies and stargazers. Kisses Monk, the cat. And Vincent, that mad dog, and even Bosco in his backyard in Rosedale. She sends a special kiss to Allen, in his eternal longing, next to the espresso machine. Kisses Professor Wylie for his activism, even though the sixties are dead. Kisses her mother and those who danced with her. She blows a kiss goodbye to the manager of the liquor store, standing in the alley, his pants down around his ankles. Kisses Louis Ciel. Blows a kiss to the golden-haired Dorvier children and their beautiful, gold-encrusted mother. Holds Grace in a secret embrace. Even Roxy and Charlie get kissed on the mouth. And Jerry gets a big kiss, trapped in the elevator. She even kisses my old boss, crying in his office next to an empty safe. And she kisses my wounded ankle, and we make love and drink wild cups of Italian coffee.

I film her secrets. I know this because I've watched her sleeping and am watching her now. And with these night visions, she turns blue. Her skin, a soft blue. Her face, blue. Her thin neck, blue. Shoulders, blue. Breasts, blue. Hands, arms, belly, legs, blue. Her lips, dark blue. I can see it in the film because in it she only sleeps in the nude. Even clothed, she's naked, like a Matisse nude—the one he shaped after he went blind. Remembering curves under his hands; a child playing at building a world. Picking it up piece by piece and setting it down to shape an image. We, too, are children playing, but mad with our inability to make anything move. From this madness, we play at destroying art. We play at denying beauty, and start with ourselves. Eat away at our body parts. Sleep awake. Ravage our bodies and ruin our voices. Poison our words and call it a vision. Search for a drug and take all things as drugs to numb the senses, control the drives, shield the womb. Never daring to touch the earth with bare feet. We devote ourselves to anything but the world. And if there is no light in darkness, no kindness without madness, then yes, I'm alone when I watch this film. Without Penelope to order me to stop dreaming. Fin.

Another Suicide Bombing

...TEN...

George slurped down the runny, sunny-side-up eggs his mother Dolores had made for him. He stepped into his Kodiak work boots and headed out to the sperm bank over by the bowling alley. Exhausted, he hadn't slept that night or any other night that month; and, since it was the middle of the month, George began to worry. The dark circles he kept under his eyes had become bags. Ash. A haze had developed over everything he saw. Insomnia was real. He'd tried pills, teas, and sprays in vain. Now, he accepted his current ailment and told no one. Now, he did what he could to go on, and he longed for sleep and silence.

...NINE...

Of the three sperm banks that he knew of, George had reached the donation limit at all but one of them. He had been a devout and disciplined donor for a year and a half, never missing his weekly appointments. He donated religiously, not only to earn extra money—finding some physical release—but also to satisfy his overwhelming urge to pass on his genes. He felt assured that with the amount of his sperm in circulation, he was bound to father a child or two eventually, if he hadn't already done so. On his information file, he passed himself off as a former Olympic middleweight boxer turned executive with a passion for concertos in B minor. He also stipulated that he was never to meet up with the woman on the receiving end, or with any children produced. George understood that he was down to his last bank and that his donating days were numbered. He considered the possibility of giving blood, but hated the sight of the stuff.

George was given a cup and a stack of gentlemen's magazines and he entered a tiny, white, low-lit room. He unattached his coveralls and sat exposed, staring at the wall. He decided on Barely Legal Fully Bare Teens and dropped the rest of the stack to the floor. Nothing happened. Slumped on his stool, grimacing and straining for ten minutes, George couldn't blame the young Latina that stared back at him off the page. He wanted to cry, but no tears would come. He dressed, gathered the magazines and empty cup, and went looking for a nurse.

He told Lorraine that he didn't want to donate today. She took him at his word as a former Olympian. She liked George and saw in him more than what the other nurses saw. She was unmarried, in her late thirties, and shy, but felt comfortable around him. She liked the fact that he never looked her in the eye and mumbled when he spoke, as she did. They had gone out together once to the bowling alley across the street. Since then, she had desperately wanted a second date. It was set. George agreed to take her to the carnival the following night. He usually declined her offers, but he badly wanted out of the clinic and couldn't think of an excuse fast enough. He told her he'd meet her there and set off to work at the meatpacking plant.

...EIGHT...

George finished his shift and went home. There was no more meat to pack today. He entered his mother's house and found her mopping up water from the bathroom floor. Somewhere a pipe was clogged. He went to the freezer and threw in the two kilos of wrapped ground beef that he had brought home from work. There had always been frozen ground beef in the freezer: his father had brought it home for thirty years before he died last spring, and now George brought it home.

He changed and told his mother he would take another look at the pipe after he finished his heaping pile of shepherd's pie. He ate his dinner in silence and didn't let on that the pie was burnt. He knew his mother must have left it in too long as she attended to the mess in the bathroom. He ate the whole pie—every bit of burnt corn, smashed potato, and ground beef—without so much as a grimace and washed it down with some warm, slightly soured milk.

...SEVEN...

It was a clogged pipe just out of George's reach in the back of the toilet that was causing the trouble. He went fiercely at the toilet with the plunger until he was red in the face. Flushed. Thrust the plunger back into the bowl, panting, and pumped again. The floor was wet. George fell to his knees, but he held in his cry. He got up and flushed again. Water gushed from out of the toilet and down onto the floor and through George's blue socks. He flushed again and again, jiggling the knob and driving the plunger down hard until the water held. He mopped up, changed, and threw his socks into a hamper by the door.

George listened to Dizzy Gillespie until his mother fell asleep. He himself had played trumpet in his high school band. Now, his rusted horn hung out in the garage. It had not been blown for a good seventeen years.

George felt his body protesting against the shepherd's pie among other things, and thought of his favourite late night neighbourhood diner: Greasy Tony's. They had a limited but reliable menu of onion rings, French fries, whistle dogs, and burgers.

...SIX...

George sat down at an empty booth and ordered one of each. It was his nightspot, the place where he had been spending many sleepless nights. He was an awesome eater and could down meal after meal, and he often would. He consumed Tony's greasy entrées and pushed the thought of his mother finding him there out of his mind. George stared at his empty plate and felt a great pressure building in his lower abdomen. He reached into his coat pocket and retrieved a brown paper bag. Out of the bag, he pulled a container of Rolaids and ripe prunes wrapped in cellophane. He consumed a few of each and put the bag back inside his coat. Perhaps tonight was the night.

George's bowels were in a knot. He sat in the back restroom of Greasy Tony's and held back a drone. Two long, drawn out weeks were too long to go without relief. He was constipated. He found a rolled up newspaper under his trousers and leafed through it. The headline of a story on page six read: "Another Suicide Bombing." It told of an 18-year-old Palestinian girl who blew herself up at a Jerusalem supermarket. George stared at the face of the young girl who had taken her own life and the life of another, and didn't move. He didn't understand the story. He didn't understand what was going on in the Middle East. He read about but couldn't picture the bomb that the girl had strapped to herself, made of explosives and nails. He dropped the paper on the bathroom floor and tried to cry. He made no sound and there were no tears. He let nothing out.

George got up and out of the bathroom stall and superficially washed his hands. He noticed his reflection in the mirror for what felt like the first time in a very long time. He looked the same as in all the pictures on his mother's living room walls, only now he was puffy, swollen, worn. His hair was almost grey. His face, red and blotchy. His shirt clung to him and his pants were rolled around under his stomach. He didn't recognize himself. George panicked. He looked down to his hands. They were swollen too. His feet hurt. His back, his teeth, his neck, his ears, his armpits—everything ached. He could see his heart beating under the skin in every part of his body. A vein on his forehead moved up and down. His thighs tingled. He didn't feel human.

...FIVE...

Blood trickled down George's wrist as he hung a forty-kilo slab of beef on the rack. The plant felt colder and wetter today than usual. He only worked part-time but figured that he'd have to work extra hours now that he couldn't donate sperm. He thought about his upcoming date with Lorraine and if he should tell his mother about it. She would be happy. A whistle blew.

...FOUR...

Dolores knew that her son had trouble with women, but was overjoyed at the prospect of the date. She told him that she would try to fix the toilet tonight, and for him to go and lie down after dinner. The shepherd's pie wasn't burnt today. She ironed one of her late husband's dress shirts and laid out one of his old suits for George to wear.

George put on a Dizzy Gillespie album and lay down. The bed sank under his body. George closed his eyes and tried to imagine his life away. He imagined that he was a song—a song that everybody loved and would hum to when it came on. He imagined that he was the smell of warm bread on a Sunday afternoon, that he was a shade of moonlight that could be seen only on clear, crisp nights, or the very last tip of the sun that lingered before it set. He imagined that he was the fresh air in the sheets when hung out on the clothesline. Or the curves of a Matisse nude. That he was a child's laugh. A lover's moan. And the first and last breath of every person everywhere ever born. He imagined himself being all of these things and fell fast asleep.

...THREE...

His mother woke him up twenty minutes later, excited. He squeezed himself into his dead father's shirt and suit and combed his knotted hair. In the mirror, his swollen face stared back at him. George wasn't sure if he had truly slept. He wondered if he'd imagined that too. His mother made a corsage out of flowers from the backyard and showed George how to pin the flowers onto Lorraine when he saw her.

Lorraine took the flowers from George's engorged hand and pinned them on herself. She had dressed up too. She wore a white dress with frills on the collar and around the hem. The two walked through the carnival—through the crowds of children and the shouts of midway attendants—and almost held hands. George kept his head down, but Lorraine held hers slightly higher. She carried a kind of excitement with her. They bought cotton candy. And George ate two waffle ice creams as well. They barely spoke.

The Ferris wheel operator pressed the safety bar down hard into George's belly and over their laps. Music played as the ride began slowly. Lorraine reached over and wrapped her arms around George's arm. The wind blew through their hair. George almost felt free, strapped in tightly, being held onto so high in the air. He considered telling Lorraine everything.

...TWO...

But she spoke instead. She told George that she was lonely. That she didn't understand life. How her thirty-six years had passed her by in a flash, and now a fog clouded everything. She told him that she didn't know who she was or where she was going. How lately she was having trouble sleeping. Lorraine told George she wanted a child, someone to go on after she was gone. Lorraine told George that she had chosen him as the donor-father in her artificial insemination. She told him that she was expecting their baby.

The Ferris wheel had picked up speed and was now at full velocity. George felt a great pressure growing inside of him. He trembled as he went up and down and around and around. He felt dizzy. And the pressure inside moved throughout his body. A button on his father's shirt popped off. He was swelling visibly. His body pulsed with every heartbeat. The bucket they sat in began to shake. All the liquid that was George wanted out. He was expanding. There was nothing he could do about it. Calmly, George forced his swollen hand to his lips and blew a kiss to the world.

...ONE...

George blew up and rained down on the carnival that night in cascading sheets of white, brown, and red—every bit of burnt corn, smashed potato, ground beef, and warm, slightly soured milk. He rained down—like a sperm bank, like a meatpacking plant, like a rolled up newspaper or a men's magazine, like onion rings and whistle dogs, like a song that everyone can hum, like the smell of warm bread on a Sunday afternoon, like a shade of moonlight on a clear, crisp night, like the last tip of the lingering sun before it sets, like clean, white sheets on a clothesline, like the curves of a Matisse nude, like a child's laugh, like a lover's groan, like the birth cry and the last breath of every person ever born, like Dizzy Gillespie and his horn, like the baby in Lorraine's womb, like his mother and father, like another suicide bomber in Jerusalem.

Unpublished

I'm staring at a tiny elephant paperweight on Donnelly's desk. Beside it are two wooden picture frames. One picture is of his German shepherd, Robert, and the other is of him with his wife and son. He's an intense-looking man with a great shock of white hair and bushy eyebrows that don't quite match. His wife is a pinkish, kind-looking lady with an enormous smile. The young boy, his son, has short, brown hair matted on his forehead. His bangs cover his eyes. Freckles cover his face, which appears contorted for the shot. I find it hard to look at him and quickly grab my notebook. This is what I write down:

> I'm asking,
> Just asking, who is gonna
> touch the ugly kid?
> You?
> Me neither.

Donnelly enters his office and sits down at his desk.

"What are you writing there?" he asks.

"Poem."

"A poem? Good. Always be writing. That's the only way to get better."

I can tell by his tone that he is not going to include my story in the Alumni Journal.

"The only way to succeed in writing is to persevere, son. Press on. Never give it up. There is no substitution for life experience, either. I have been putting pen to paper for thirty years. 'Time is the great emancipator.'"

He quotes from one of his own compositions.

"What about my story?" I ask. He looks puzzled. I persist. "The one I submitted for the magazine last month."

His face grows pale. "I don't remember the story," he says. "Are you sure that you gave it to me?" He pauses. Then buries his face in his hands. "Oh yes, your story. I forgot about your story. I remember it now."

He apologizes and tries to humour me with anecdotes about his premature senility. "I'm afraid that I am going to have to pass on your submission. Your story is too vague, I'm afraid, not enough life experience there. And why you felt you had to stick poems in the story, I'll never understand. They didn't quite work. It's just not for us. But it'll come, mark my words, it'll come."

I always feel empty leaving Donnelly's office. He has a way of making me feel hopeless. I push him out of my mind and focus on the fact that the story is finished; the break is much needed. There are other things I want to write.

It's late and I'm on my way home. Out of cigarettes, all I have are my thoughts to ward off the cold. But they won't. They never do. I pass a homeless man wrapped in a rag of a sleeping bag, dreaming of kindness and beer. I pass a pizza place that sells cheap slices that smell great and almost tempt me to go in. But I am already on the stairs of the Queen Street subway station stop. The coins in my pocket are cold and lost in a hole in the lining of my coat. Three dollars will take me wherever I want to go.

I throw the change in the box, push through the turnstile, and blend into rush hour. I smile at the thought of rarely ever working: I write when I feel like it. The platform is not busy yet. I check to see where I'm going: southbound. An old Chinese man sees me and goes up against a wall. The sound is loud underground, and wind blows hard. The draft stinks, but is warm. Doors open. People get out and rush toward the cold outside. I get on and stand by the door. We go. I see my reflection in a window. Young. Cold. Tired. My hair is wild. Good. My collar looks good up with a red scarf around my neck. Pushed up against a pole, I sway with the train. We stop. People get off. Others get on. We go again. I see myself in the tinted glass. Sway, stop. People get off. Others get on.

Squeezed in tightly, staring at me with heavily made-up eyes, there's a woman sitting close to me. She's almost staring right through me. She's forty-five. She could be fifty. Her hair is long and blonde and almost white and tied back above her head. She wears a faded, white wool coat with faded fur around the collar and sleeves. Her hands are long and thin and chapped from the cold. She holds a soft leather bag on her lap. She turns her face away from mine and searches for a prop, a comb, lipstick, a tiny mirror. The show is for me. The entire cast riding south, all for me. I am lost in her hair and the lines in her face. She keeps looking at me. Who the hell is that? Who the hell is he?

She crosses and uncrosses her legs. She lets her hair down; it falls soft on her slender shoulders. I stare at her. She looks up. I turn away. She stares at me. I look up. She turns away.

At the next stop, a crowd rushes in: loud, bored, boars. Rush hour crowd going home with their blue-suit office talk. I open up my notebook and try to take dictation. I take it down as I hear it: "If he would just do something, anything, I don't care what, send a goddamned e-mail, brew some goddamned coffee—but no. Type a damn memo, make a few calls, something. Hold the damn elevator, kiss my damned ass. What the hell are we paying you to do? Nothing or something? I tell ya, some of these guys don't know their ass from their armpit."

I lose her in the crowd. Lose sight of my reflection in the window. Lose sight of the suits and of Donnelly in his office. I'm some unknown someone underground with the crowd, but all alone. Whose fantasy is this?

I feel a hand run across my back, and it's not the hand of the asshole in the blue suit. And I feel the hand come around my back and find my hand holding the pole. And it's not the hand of the homeless man begging for a buck. And I feel a hand sliding down touching my hand. And it's not the hand of Donnelly's ugly kid. And I feel the hand, and I feel the hand. And I feel her asking me to get off and go with her at the next stop. This is what I write down in my notebook:

The call went out to let wonder take over
And so the boy let wonder take over
for his senses were numbed in the face of purity
And the promise of perfection
the prophetic dream
it seemed
had shocked longing unconscious
that beautifully suffocated all who watched
but the boy only gazed up
and gave up
in recognition of the realization
and let wonder take over

She lives in a house on the corner of Islington and Celina: number 14B. She unlocks the door and a hungry cat runs to her; she calls him Bonzo. The poverty of the place is real: there are dishes in a sink, an unmade bed in the center of the room, clothes on the floor. I breathe in deeply, looking for my life experience. She pours wine into a plastic cup and laughs that she doesn't know my name. She kisses me hard on the mouth with perfect, cracked lips. I see her face differently now: close-up and real. She has tiny bruises under her eyes. She calls them her beauty marks and asks me to kiss them.

"Don't think I'm crazy," she says and asks me if I've ever been to skid row before.

I tell her I haven't. She tells me that I look like her son. She laughs and pours more wine. Then says that I look nothing like him; and leafs through my notebook without looking at the pages.

"What's this? Homework?" She laughs again and throws the book under the bed.

We almost make love.

"Don't leave," she says. "Say that you'll stay."

And she tells me she's sorry for the state of her room and for the tiny stubble on her thin, bare legs.

"I didn't know I'd be dancing tonight," she says.

And she jumps up wildly and tells me that I'm beautiful. And throws her arms around me and sways like the subway, drunk. And she cries. And I stay. And she falls asleep, or simply passes out. Her head against my chest. And Bonzo comes and stretches out on her hair. I reach down under the bed, looking for my book. This is what I want to write down:

Stay gloriously high in praise
and deliver joy to those of us
who can only praise you,
and offer you passage in
blinding the audience—
taunting them on stilts—
naked sailor of the mind—
too close to let the waves take us,
too far off in the distant mist.
Stop saving the misfits,
feeding them tea and biscuits,
as we wait with our sacred longing
for your applause

There's a noise at the door that makes the cat jump. I lie still under her, and can't move. A man dressed in a worn leather coat, carrying a big, brown paper bag, comes through the door, unannounced, and stands by the bed. He takes in the scene, and then lets out a laugh. He claps his hands loudly again and again. He grabs the hair of the woman sleeping on top of me; she lets out a little scream as she wakes up.

"Who the hell is this?" he asks her. Her face is inches away from his. "Some kid looking for a thrill? And you, drunk and in his arms. This room is private, right, baby? This is a honeymoon suite, isn't it, baby?"

She falls to the ground and laughs and laughs in a high pitch. I'm off the bed now and into my coat. I can't find my shoes.

"And where are you off to, lover?" he asks. He slaps me hard on the back of my head. "There's nothing free in this life!"

He slaps me again and tells me to give over any money I have. He takes my handful of change and a crumpled-up five dollar bill and throws it to his lady on the ground. Her eyes are rolled back in her head and her body trembles with each laugh she lets out. She keeps calling his name:

"Dirk," she says, "Dirk, Dirk."

I'm pushed out the door, and feel it slam behind me. The radiator buzzes in the hall. I'm gone. Life experience, my ass.

I'm going home. The subway train lets me off, and I head for my apartment on the corner of Bedford and Dupont. The TV is on. There's a half-eaten bowl of popcorn on the table. It's the last few minutes of the hockey game. I stick my hand into the bowl of popcorn and sit down on the couch. The announcer describes in detail each goal, each penalty and bad decision so far in the game. He describes the two fights in the second period and how you're gonna lose money on this one, if you're a betting man. I sit and watch the game and eat popcorn, and try to stop my hands from shaking. I want to write something in my notebook. I know exactly what I want to write. But I don't have it with me. So I can't write it down in my book. And since I didn't leave it in Donnelly's office, and since I didn't leave it on the subway, I know where I left it. Under the bed, where Dirk and his lady are probably lying in each others' arms, making love or counting change, or reading the stories and poems in my notebook in the honeymoon suite in that house in the city's west end.

Change Room

At that time, I was thirty years old and district manager of a fast food joint now long since gone under. Working my way up for years, I'd become the assistant fryer at fifteen, then a full-fledged fryer, then cashier, floor maintenance, drive-thru, junior manager, assistant manager and, eventually, district manager. Ambitious teen turned youngest district manager Burger World had ever seen. There must be a plaque hanging somewhere with the entire history engraved on it.

It was Friday. I'd almost done my rounds. Once a day, I visited each store in my district. Checked policy, group cheer, proper deposits. I was just getting over a huge bust, which had me in good standing with head office. I'd brought down a senior manager who'd been skimming off the top. It was a bittersweet victory, though. Seeing a fat, balding, middle-aged man bawling his eyes out and begging to stay with the company scared me at first, but then made me sad. The only other time I'd seen a

grown man cry was at my grandfather's funeral.

That night, it was raining. I was speeding to my last store. Frustration mixed with fatigue. Someone had been paging me for the past three hours, and it was getting on my nerves. Timmy Swino had managed the place for the past six years. I knew him to be a trustworthy, reliable man. I was sure that Ed Stock, his excitable, effeminate assistant manager must have lost his cool. Or maybe they were low on buns. Ed had rushed me in once before because a group of drunk youngsters had threatened to burn the place down if they didn't get free onion rings. After ten years, I was numb to men like Ed.

When I pulled into the parking lot, I saw some employees huddled together out front in the rain. I remember thinking I'd probably have to replace all their paper hats now that they were drenched.

Idiots, I thought, even as I crossed the yellow police tape.

"Mr. Layman!"

"Stay back, girls."

I explained who I was to a cop at the door and pushed by the group, mostly sixteen-year-old girls working part-time. There was an extra large number of them there because the shifts were about to change. Their tears filled me more with contempt than concern. The place was empty. Someone had shut off the grill and fry machine. There was commotion down the back hallway that led to the storage room, the washrooms, and the staff change rooms. The words—Guys and Dolls—were written on the doors.

Ed was sitting at the front booth. His hair was wild. His eyes, red and puffy. He had his jacket off. The sleeves of his cheap, striped dress shirt were rolled up to the elbows. I made a mental note of how out-of-uniform he looked.

"Are you all right, Ed?" I asked.

He remained still, lost in thought.

"Ed, what the hell happened here?"

"Oh, Charlie, Charlie," he said, coming to. Then he rubbed his eyes, trying to hide the fact that he'd been crying.

"C'mon, Ed. You all right?"

"I'm fine," he said. "Oh, Charlie, I've been calling and I knew you'd be coming but..."

"Never mind that," I said. "What the hell happened?"

Ed grew more and more frantic as he described the incident. It had been a normal open and afternoon shift. Ed had opened the floor, and Tim was working the office.

"We were getting ready for the change-over, and Tim said he needed to take a breather coz he wasn't feeling well," explained Ed.

The story seemed well rehearsed. I imagined he must have told it at least nine times already.

"It was Ziggy who found him," he said. "He came in for the evening shift and went in to get changed."

He broke down as he described finding Tim on the floor.

"Buckets of blood, Charlie! Buckets of blood."

He seemed keen on that phrase.

"The paramedics said he had an aneurysm. Blood everywhere."

The image sickened me a little. For the first time, I took notice of Ziggy, alone in the corner.

"How is he?" I asked.

"Dead, Charlie! Dead on impact."

"Not Tim. Ziggy."

He looked over and seemed to notice Ziggy for the first time, too. Just then a huge cop approached and began questioning me. He went over the same story, but with less emotion, and said that Swino had been pronounced dead on arrival. I filled him in on what I knew about the deceased. It wasn't much. I knew a few things. The cop took me into the boys' change room, now sectioned off by police tape. Wet blood was all over the floor. I noted how the colour resembled the extra tubs of ketchup stored next to the lockers.

"Poor bastard," remarked the cop.

More questions from other cops followed. And then more forms. Everything seemed under control. The rain had cleared a little. I went back outside. Told our employees to go home and relax for the time being, but to report for their next shift. The twin sisters, hired two weeks before, seemed horrified. I felt awkward around them. I noticed the way their two-toned uniform shirts clung tightly to their small breasts.

Ed had not moved since my arrival. I told him to go home and rest. Thanked him as best I could for handling the situation. That seemed to satisfy him; that sort of thing always satisfies men like Ed.

"Oh, Charlie," he said, getting up. "Claire and the kids, uh, we haven't been able to contact Claire yet."

Claire was Swino's wife of eighteen years. They had three children. I bit down hard and told him I'd take care of it. He said he knew I would and left, satisfied.

Only a few cops stayed around now and one very important-looking paramedic. By then, the cops were on autopilot and talked about their wives and the Blue Jays. They paid no attention to me. So I went in to wash my face and hands. I felt dirty. When I opened the door to the washroom, the sight of Ziggy's stone face in the mirror scared the hell out of me.

"Zig," I said coolly, "you've had a tough day. Go home."
I felt bad for the kid. Staring at the mirror, Ziggy remained in his trance.

"Zig!" I repeated.

"Mr. Layman," he said without moving, "I have to tell you something."

His dramatics annoyed me. I wasn't interested in the kid's mental shrinkage. "What is it?"

"Not until they leave," he said steadily.

"Just tell me."

"Not until they leave," he insisted.

I figured he must have had a day to remember and told him I understood. I grabbed a coffee from behind the counter and waited on the paramedic back in the change room, which was now clean.

"That guy had one hell of a fall," the paramedic said. "Jesus! What a way to go." He seemed engrossed in his note taking. I did my best to move him along with a smirk and a nod.

"Buckets of blood," he muttered.

He left soon after that. And then the cops left. The scene was too unreal for me to realize how late it was. Ziggy had drifted back to the front and looked the same as before. I went after the facts.

"Ziggy, is there something you want to say?"

He looked through me.

"Yes."

He led me over to the change room. Guys written on the door.

"I did something in here before the police came," he said.

"What?"

My tone was changing. He hesitated.

"I had to do it," he said and began to cry.

"What?"

I resented being led on by a fifteen-year-old kid.

"He has three young daughters," he said, talking around me.

"Just tell me what the hell happened," I persisted.

"I came in to change and Mr. Swino was on the floor and there was all this blood around him and this pop crate."

Ziggy pulled a two-foot-high, wooden crate back into position, re-enacting the scene.

"And?"

The kid stood up on the crate and raised his hands over his head.

"The ceiling tile was pulled back like this."

He was thrilled and horrified at his discovery.

"You can see right into the girls' change room!"

He was crying as he reached up and moved the tile back to where it had been. To make sure of what he was saying, I went next door to the adjoining room, Dolls. A thin wall separated the two change rooms. When I looked up, I noticed there was an opening in the ceiling.

Peeping Tim, I thought. I wondered if he'd seen the twins.

I felt like the guy from Public Works who cleans up the road kill. I deposited the day's accounts. Double-checked the grill. Turned out the lights, the words Burger World still flashing on the sign in the parking lot, and offered Zig a ride home.

"Sorry the car is such a mess," I said, rolling up a porn magazine I had on the front seat and putting it in the glove compartment. I reached into my shirt pocket, pulled out a couple of coupons for free fries and passed them to Ziggy. The way I looked at it, he would eventually have to eat something. He took the coupons without saying a word. I turned on the radio and drove him home.

Honeymoon at the Falls

It was all about the ring: the diamond, two carats. And the year and a half engagement upon a seven-year wait through high school and college. And June, the perfect time for a wedding, if the sun would shine. And it would. And the perfect bride: Lily— gold ringlets falling over her slender shoulders and down to the small of her back. Sweetheart. And the perfect bridegroom: Peter—tall, dark, ambitious. Realist. And a plan that was airtight, any young couple's dream of a home together, built on her work at the hospital and his at the bank. And leanings towards children. Two, maybe three. And a dog one day, if Peter was lucky. And a promise to stay together, close to their families, and live for love, for health and in safety; to make a place for themselves out of the chaos and the horror of the world around them. And with the world around them not being so bad, not so, so bad in their southern Ontario town, if anyone could do it, could pull it off, it was the two of them. Best friends getting through tough times together in adolescent uncertainty. Mini-

breakdowns and sad, jealous nights. Habits hard to kick. Everything
conquered. Counselling in their freshmen year apart. A tolerance now
for football and goodwill towards the films of Harrison Ford.

Lily's parents, Jackie and Ed, and Peter's folks, Beatrice and
Arthur, were all thrilled at the union. Retired, North American living
furthering the convenience of the affair. A modest event in the sanctity
of St. James United Church on the corner of Capri and Redgrove.
Ninety people. Compromises made on the list. Friends, family, and a
conscious effort to separate the feuding guests on the dinner's seating
plan. Chicken cordon bleu. And old Auntie Winnie out for the day.
Flowers from Van Belles. Long coattail tuxes. Three bridesmaids. All
the ladies-in-waiting ready to put on yet another faded, almost pink
dress. And the wedding gown itself, Lily's gown, pure white, of course.
No foul play. No shotgun necessary, or sulking in the basement of the
church. An added anticipation of the honeymoon in Niagara Falls for
three weeks to come.

No one was to talk about the bachelor party, or the shower for
the bride. A last chance to let go completely; to be completely free
from one another, alone with the boys or with the girls. The men, in
a rented Greyhound bus that the best man, Donald, would drive (the
only sober one of the group) hopping from one Zanzibar to another.
Whipped cream and pool tables. And pools of vomit and other fluids
on the floor of the bathroom. Lily's brother, Charlie, would push
the images of Peter on that night out of his head and accept him as
anyone would. The brother-in-law he always wanted. Finally a fellow
golfer in the family. Or for the women, gifts, all of them edible. Male
parts or underwear that shocked the older ladies sitting in wooden
chairs around the living room. Shocked, yes, but not too, too much.

And they all moved in. The whole group. Awkward in Sunday
best. And some quite funny in hairdressing disasters. And the look
on Ed's face at the top of the aisle said it all—the one who paid for
the whole damn thing. After a metronome parade of ushers and
bridesmaids who had always wanted to be in just such a church
play—this ritual. Just like Peter, convinced at the last moment to
wear ladies' foundation makeup on his face.

"For the pictures," she said.

Peter stood now, proud, and stared down the long aisle at his
soon-to-be wife, soon-to-be partner. And he had to face it and he
would, lover. Who doesn't cry at a wedding? And who proves himself
to be the ultimate ham-actor—bringing out the best or the worst in

people. Lily looked the best. Always the bride who looks best. The bride's day. And the flare-up, the rash that appeared on the right side of her face four weeks before, from anxiety or nerves, was gone now, turned pure—white like her dress, which fit well. She looked well. Good enough to eat. And if only he didn't have to concentrate on remembering his lines—the vows he had memorized—Peter would be concentrating on that fact.

The minister began. And most tuned out or stayed tuned in to the things that truly interested them most. Uncle Vernon's new digital camera. How lovely the church looked. Memories of past weddings. Questions like: When will I be married? When are we going to eat? When will I get to honeymoon at the Falls? All thoughts on themselves. The congregation meaning well, but unable to switch the focus from the self—which is natural and normal and best illustrated at gatherings such as this—June 10th, 1:30 p.m.

Wedded bliss, papers signed, a father-present church-kiss. A blur to the couple, but a full forty-five minute scene, especially for the children present. Cousins, new nephews and nieces, who all looked so nice or at least clean. Rice and pictures in the garden of the city's biggest mansion house. A Garden of Eden. Paradise. Like the rented limos parked out front, pushing the limits of class they fell into. Pushing the middle to upper in their middle-class passports. The combination of photographs elaborate and all possibilities worked out for wallet size and full 8X10 and an album to come. Complete after the pictures from the honeymoon had been taken and developed. The camera's flash—unrelenting, unforgiving—forging this moment into history. No candid shots, only posed and controlled freeze frames. "And burn the unflattering pics—red eyes, twitching eyes shut, too much face, too much chin."

A line formed to meet the two, to meet Lily and Peter for the first time now as man and wife. En route to the love feast, the banquet in the lower dining hall at the Sheridan Hotel. Everything going as planned. All things moving well as planned. "Can you believe it? And yes this reminds me of our high school senior prom." Everyone relaxed now, having given over to whatever they were wearing and the heat of the day and the anticipation of the food. The wet bar tended by Bill, the new minister, the administrator in charge now of the party portion of the event. And the drinks were all pre-paid and made to make for an interesting dance after supper and speeches. The DJ's request list cross-referenced and balanced to the frequency of

the time and place. But the newlyweds—strict. Eating well. But small
amounts. No drinking. Conservative dancing. Maybe join in the conga
line and offer one showpiece for the sake of Unchained Melody. All to
conserve energy and spirit and keep up appearances for what was to
come: their first day and night together. A life to lead.

And glasses were raised and toasts made. Some more eloquent
than others, based on the speaker's willingness and wit. The banging
of the plates and "not too tight or you'll spoil her dress." The fuss
over the cake had yielded a beautiful dessert. Three storeys of icing.
A tiny, perfect man and wife on top. An incredible miniature likeness
above a castle of flour and frosting and delicious anticipation, but for
God's sake keep the children's fingers away. Until the groom stood for
the final toast.

"To my wife. To our life together. May she find all the happiness
in the world with me, in spite of all my annoying little habits and my
bad memory, and my bad breath in the morning and the problems I
bring home with me from the bank and the bets I'm sure to lose on
the next fifteen Super Bowls to come and my horrible sense of style."
(The guests applauded.) "May she hold up through it all and bear
with me. And praise God she chose me. The love of my life, my best
friend, my partner, my beautiful woman." (More applause.) "Just
remember, honey, I'm only human."

At that, they all rose and applauded and cheered and the DJ
began the first song. Mr. and Mrs. Peter and Lily Rance took the floor
and danced the evening into night where, after a short train ride, they
found themselves in the honeymoon suite of a tiny B & B in Niagara
Falls, Ontario.

The room was quite obviously a love den. A deep red duvet
covered a queen-sized bed with a large brass headboard and cushioned
heart pillows, sitting under a large bay window looking out to a
lush green landscape, looking through the mist and fog to the giant
waterfalls in the distance. And with a calmness and coolness about
them, they unloaded their luggage—new, matching leather gifts—
and took in the room and sipped chilled champagne. And stared out
of that bay window. And felt the seven-year wait bear down on them.
And the pressure from the morning's duties bear down on them. And
everything that is generally accepted about a man and a woman bear
down on them. And they embraced each other.

And a scrambling for the key in the lock, then the light switch
by the door, they undressed until nude. A touch of the moon came

in and danced on naked skin. They pressed their bodies against each
other and fell onto the bed, which sank under the weight of their
world. And the mouth covered the body: neck, shoulders, breasts,
nipples, ribs, bellies, thighs. And they explored each other, blind with
hands. Everything soft and breathing warm to the touch.

And it was all about making love. The romance giving over
to passion. And breathing and breathing. The heart growing like a
balloon. Everything growing. And groaning with a touch of pain that
gave over to madness, then fondness. And dancing together, entangled
and buried under each other. The body's sweetness. And the heat of
the honey rising from them—a true mist rising from deep inside their
bodies moved out of that tiny room into the summer night where the
air, thick and wet outside, embraced it and it was absorbed by the
mist of the Falls.

They lay awake in each other's arms, bodies wet, with tiny,
perfect bruises and still-swollen lips. Their eyes were hooded now and
they breathed in time together. Until, getting up, they moved in the
dark to the bathroom. Lily leading him by the hand. She turned on
the light. Eyes protested the sudden change. She got into the shower
first. Peter caught himself up in the mirror for a moment until he
followed her in. She turned on the water and tested it with delicate
fingers, adjusted the temperature. Peter's eyes adjusted to the light,
and before him, for the first time, he saw the naked body of his wife.

She leaned down and unwrapped lavender soap and held it under
the stream of the faucet. Peter stared at her from the back and saw
her spine under vanilla skin from the neck down. And she crouched
down for a moment and cupped her hands in the water and brought
it up to her body as if getting into a swimming pool. And Peter began
to tremble at the beauty of her body; at the sight of her body; at the
beauty of the woman at his feet, until he only trembled. He felt a
numbness move up from his knees to his thighs and genitals, to his
buttocks and back until he had to look away. And just as she engaged
the shower head and stood, Peter, with eyes closed now, lost himself in
the rush of that warm water falling on him, and let a stream of urine
go, just as he always did whenever he took a shower. And Lily, feeling
traces of the warmth on her back, turned slowly, softly, and faced her
wet, naked, newlywed husband. And no matter what she said to him,
he just let it flow. He wanted to stop, but didn't know how. He'd never
pissed on anybody before.

Retreat

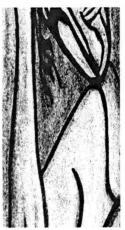

Ever since the incident with the neighbour last winter—that sudden sound of smashing glass at 3 a.m., the smell of cheap red wine, the repeated calls to 911, the Jim Morrison biography left on his doorstep, the fragmented police report, and his first-hand account of a man on PCP—Jack had become a light sleeper. He'd wake up at the slightest suggestion of a noise. If his wife, Helena, coughed, rolled over, or worse, talked in her sleep—and she was always mumbling in some kind of dream-language that he couldn't understand—Jack would bolt straight up and out of bed. It was as if he was in a constant state of watchfulness. There was only a thin veil between sleep and wakefulness for Jack, and he preferred it that way. The war stories from his father that suggested you must always sleep with one eye open in combat rang true. He was restless and ready, like a tightly coiled spring waiting to fire. Just as he was now: shooting out of the creaking bed, out from underneath the large, goose-down duvet, and landing solidly onto the hardwood floor

of the cabin.

It had been especially difficult for him to rest for the past six nights, at the northern resort located on the shore of Lake Superior. The place was remote, recessed deep inside the forest. It was, perhaps, a charming, idyllic spot for some, but the wilderness did not open up for Jack. Instead, it suffocated him. The overwhelming silence of the place, in harsh contrast to his city life, was deafening. And the cries of nature seemed to be all the more blaring because of the way they would linger and echo inside his head. The noise he heard now, the one that woke him, was a faint but persistent throbbing; the kind of sound a body makes without trying.

First, Jack leaned down over the bed and began to scrutinize Helena. It wasn't coming from her throat, although she was imperceptibly keening. He bent down closer and pressed his ear tight against her breasts, then began to drag his head down slowly the length of her torso. It sounded like the ocean beneath her skin, like listening to whale sounds inside a shell. But Jack was certain that the noise that concerned him was not from her body.

He crept out of their cold room and stood, bare chested in his boxer shorts, pricking his ears up and into the bedrooms of the other couples on retreat. Usual sleeping sounds could be heard. Somewhere, someone was snoring. Jack heard a syncopated rattle coming from the room of the large couple who shared a bad case of asthma. Somewhere, someone was passing wind, carefree. Jack heard the trace of hushed words, giggling, repentant lovemaking, and improvised singing. He stayed that way in the hall, a receiver for all the sleeping spouses. There was nothing strange about any of it. The sounds he heard did not suggest torment, or anguish, or anxiety, or even jealousy. There were no storms raging, or dying out, behind closed doors. These were the mundane marriage songs of human beings not wanting to sleep alone. The week's counselling sessions were proving to be a success, but Jack resented the calm.

He turned to go back to his room. Helena was now sprawled in the shape of a starfish, taking full advantage of the extra space in his absence. From his view by the entrance, she looked different. Jack was used to viewing Helena in close proximity: across from him at the dinner table, beside him in line at the grocery store, next to him on the couch in front of the television. But with distance between them, it was as if he were looking at someone else. He was not merely looking at his wife, but at his wife in a bed, in a room, in a cabin, in the middle of nowhere. She seemed diminished by his vantage point. She looked smaller, foreign, and he couldn't possibly know what she was dreaming about.

The image of her that morning, the one that had caused the flare-up, flashed before him again. Helena had wanted to take a canoe out for a tour of the lake. There were enough boats for each of the couples. It was after lunch and the trust exercises with Minister Bill. The other couples had all flocked to claim the best rowboats and paddle boats. Wearing matching life jackets, they shoved off and took turns steering. But Jack didn't like the look of their vessel. It was a beaten-up, red, metal canoe with two splintered paddles. The presence of an emergency bailout bucket worried him. Helena, who had been determined to make the week work, if only for herself, ignored Jack's caution, called him a spoilsport, and set out alone.

Jack tried to diminish the significance of the betrayal and wrapped himself up inside a hammock between two giant birch trees. A strong wind rocked him back and forth, as if he were a pouting child being lulled. After about ten minutes, he flipped out of his cradle, falling flat on his face against the grass, when he thought he heard the sound of his wife's call. Getting up in a daze, he looked out on the lake and saw Helena as a speck in the distance. He knew it was her because of the mass of brown curls that danced against the wind.

The lake was a moving mirror, reflecting blue and green— trees, the sky, and her. He was transfixed, watching as she paddled herself confidently around a small bank, avoiding the path of a fallen, rotting tree. Her movements were powerful as she dipped her oar into the water, raised the wood—like a wing, high above her head—and brought it down without a ripple. The woman he was staring at was no longer his wife. She was some unknown sea creature as the oblong vessel shot through the current, as if part of her body. Jack stood and peered past the stinging in his eyes until he not only no longer recognized her, but also didn't seem to know himself either. It was then that he saw it. Just as she turned to disappear around a patch of maples, Jack saw the distinct outline of another body inside her canoe.

The episode was later recounted by Helena, who had returned from the voyage a rejuvenated woman, as another hallucination. But Jack had not imagined it. This other body was broad and looming. It was perfectly balanced on the water. Its head emerged from its shoulders with upward certainty, stooping slightly in the shape of a large, black question mark with a robust torso and an angular, muscled back. Though its presence was heavy inside his mind's eye, Jack understood the form to be as light and transitory as any apparition.

Helena morphed from starfish to seahorse as she tossed in her sleep and, clutching her pillow, assumed the foetal position. Curled and alone in the massive bed, she now looked like the child that they could not conceive. At that moment, Jack wanted to pick her up in his arms and hold her against his body. He wanted to run with her like that in his arms out of the cabin, through the forest of dying trees, all the way back to the city. But the throbbing sound that had woken him stirred him once again, as Helena became herself and continued to sleep in peace. Jack was determined to find it now. He slipped down the hall past the others to the main entrance of the cabin and peered out a window. The night was black, except for the moon. The cabin faced the lake, but Jack could not differentiate between the water and the land. He could barely perceive where the sky overtook the landscape. He retrieved Minister Bill's flashlight by the door and went outside.

It was no longer a throbbing, although he could now hear his heart in his head. The sound was less human, closer to a rapid flutter. It was clearly coming from the dock. Jack aimed the flashlight in front of him, in the vague direction of the water, which was no longer reflecting anything. He advanced, stumbling past the discarded game of horseshoes, the barbecue pit, and the makeshift campfire that he had not attended. He had no bearings now and only knew that he was close to the shore because of the feel of wet sand under his bare feet.

The fluttering mounted as he drew in closer. It became wet and frenetic. Jack frantically searched with his flashlight, determined to silence the spasm. Entering the water fully, moving past the chill up to his waist, the noise consumed him until without warning, it stopped. The shock of silence forced him off his feet and pulled him under. Water filled up inside his ears, eyes, and mouth. Jack understood that he was drowning. But he wasn't, because he had already re-emerged, gasping for air and gauging the depth. He raised his arms high above his head. The blackness of the night opened up before him and he saw, without doubt, the looming form from Helena's canoe.

It stood over him on land: looming, menacing, watching. Jack threw himself at it with all the force of his trembling body. The creature did not retreat, and seemed to surrender to Jack's repeated blows with the flashlight. He struck out against its monstrous head and long, twisting legs and feet that clawed at his bare ankles, knees, and thighs. It was marking him, even as he was killing it. Jack could not imagine how much damage a flashlight could do. Grunting and squawking, they wrestled together. In an instant, Jack glimpsed the shape of a shadowy wingspan on the ground with its long flight feathers and dark plume. He heard its bitter croak.

He managed to lift the colossal bird over the side of a canoe without capsizing it. Then untying the rope that secured it to the dock, he began paddling, in circles at first, until he found some kind of rhythm, and was able to cut an awkward zigzag through the black water. He had to get rid of it, but didn't know whether or not it would float.

Turning back to gauge how far out they'd gone, Jack saw the outline of his wife, Helena, standing on the shore. She may have been shouting and calling his name, but Jack heard nothing. Although he couldn't bear any more shame in front of her, and he didn't know what to do with the bird, she would. As Jack tried feebly to turn the canoe around, the large bird he had wrestled on the bank lifted out of the canoe and flew upwards towards the shore. Helena saw Jack paddling with tremendous force, while over his head rose the plumed shadow of the Great Blue Heron.

Spice Up Your Life

Frank and Stella Martin receive a book for their thirtieth wedding anniversary. The book is entitled, *How to Spice Up Your Life in the Bedroom*. Friends are roaring inside the couple's two-storey brick house in the east end of the city.

"Now whose one is this?" Stella is laughing.

"That'll do, eh, Frank?" Gregor, the couple's attorney and long-time friend, is snarling. "Old dogs—new tricks!"

The bloated pack carries on in this way: cheeks red and noses bulbous. They're gorging themselves on sherry served in snifters and large Martha's Piggies-in-a-Blanket. All the ladies—wearing pastel polyester pantsuits—hold their guts, prop themselves up on the uncomfortable living room couches, and take turns skimming through the naughty book. Passing it around the room, they smudge the pages with greasy fingers until Stella places it absently beside the new slow cooker and glistening 9-iron. The couples sing rehearsed karaoke. And even though the Noakes are drunk,

they remember their choreography. It's not long before everybody forgets about the how-to guide. Everybody but Frank.

Frank can't shake the shame. He can't get his mind off it. Although he shows no outward signs, he's inwardly seething. The couples are busy viewing pictures on the big screen of the Martins' recent trip to Germany. Frank takes the opportunity to rid himself of the bad joke. Retrieves the book from the living room, tucks it down the front of his pants and under his silk shirt. Goes directly out onto the back deck where a platter of raw meat is waiting. Turns up the gas on the grill. The flame. Nearly searing off his eyebrows, the fire licks at Frank's face, nearly torching his secret hairpiece. He burns. Grabs at the obscenity in his pants. About to set the thing ablaze, when Gregor joins him.

"Meat time. Gregor like meat." His caveman impressions always come out around the barbecue.

"Frank like meat, too." Frank is feeble. "Frank make fire to cook meat." Frank's face is red. He hides the book under the platter of bloody steaks already sauced and braised.

The disappearing act works. Gregor is bleary-eyed, holding his beer up to the moon. He howls. The other men, also grown tired of pictures of Berlin, stumble out into the backyard and join in the caveman game. And by the time the women catch up with their husbands, the meat is ready for their late-night feast.

Gwendolyn, Stella's older sister, fixes plates for everyone. She has a compulsion to play hostess no matter where she goes. Tidying up, Gwendolyn finds the book. Puzzled when she sees it. Takes her a minute to process what it is. Gregor jumps up from his wooden cabana chair. Teeters.

"What's your favourite technique, Wendy?" Gregor is smeared with steak sauce.

"You're a pig," Gwendolyn snaps. "I found it by the barbecue."

"The pig position! Oinkity-oink."

"Swine."

The company roars again as before. Frank's pupils are fully dilated. He is biting his bottom lip. His nostrils are like oysters. After thirty years of marriage, Stella knows this face.

"I'll take that, thank you." And careful not to look directly at Frank, she snatches the book out of her sister's hands and pitches it over the deck's railing. "Who has room for cheesecake and charades?"

"I do. I call this the downward facing donkey." Gregor kicks off his sandals.

The guests leave around 3 a.m. Gregor is a puddle. By all accounts, it was another flawless dinner party at the Martins. Stella is so exhausted by the end of the night that she does something that she's never done in all her thirty years of married life—passes out, and falls asleep in her party dress. Frank stares at her sprawled on top of the covers. They have an agreement: always clean up directly after dinner parties, no matter how late the night goes, or how tired they may be. That way there'll be no mess in the morning—it makes sense.

Frank purses his lips. He goes down to his garage. Flicks on the light. His tan Lexus beams. He often checks up on the car before bed, but this is a different kind of mission. He's looking for his 120-watt flashlight, which he finds exactly in its place in the third drawer on the left of the utility cabinet.

Lighting a path for himself outside in the dark, Frank kicks at discarded wine bottles and paper plates. He searches the vicinity where Stella tossed the book. His grass is kept in impeccable condition and he's confident that he'll be able to locate it. But after a few minutes of grunting, he still cannot find the book. Instead, Frank discovers two raccoons hidden beneath his wooden deck. They're writhing on top of one another, eating discards from the night. Razor claws clutch bits of potato salad. The bigger of the two animals—the female—the one with the huge head, gnaws on a husk of corn.

Convinced that the raccoons have taken the book, Frank creeps to the side of his house and turns on the garden hose. Snaking it along his perfect lawn in silence, he takes aim at the filthy creatures and begins to spray. Frank has them trapped. His heart is racing as it always does when hunting. The animals chortle and it's impossible to decipher one screech from the other. Frank feels a ping in his pants as cold water drips down his forearm. He wants to drown the bastards.

Up in her room, Stella wakes up hearing animal calls. Frank is not in his bunk. Stella goes to the window and draws back burgundy curtains. She sees her husband, his feet spread wide apart and planted firmly. Water gushes from the hose's nozzle-gun. Eyes fix the target. Frank is grinding his teeth, showing them jagged and white in his opened mouth. He isn't wearing his wig. Stella stares at her husband's bald head. In all their years, she's only ever glimpsed the thing sideways in the mirror. Seeing it from above, she realizes why he keeps it hidden. It's hideous. Bigger, and terribly misshapen, like some overgrown gourd. A birthmark is splattered in maroon. Tufts of hair grow erratically. Frank is frantic—failing again. He abandons the hose, drops down to his belly. Stella loses sight of him as he writhes and wriggles his way under the wooden deck.

Frank is squeezed. Pausing a moment to listen to a wheeze in his chest, he realizes that he has no plan. It bothers him more than the fact that he's stuck. He can't get a read on the raccoons. They may have eaten the book. Or buried it. The only light in the tight spot comes from cracks of moonlight between wooden planks. Frank hears nothing beyond his own rattling pant. He digs his nails into wet earth, cold and oozing in his grip. Frank massages the muck, moulds it like potter's clay. Then, clutching a ball of mud, he tries to hurl it in the direction of the two animals.

Stella closes the curtains and takes off her party clothes. This is something that she habitually does in the dark, but on impulse, she turns on the light. Somewhat surprised at her own break in naked routine, Stella retrieves the new bottle of lavender skin lotion that her sister gave her. Systematically, Stella begins to apply the lotion to every part of her body. She does this by focusing on individual inches. First her right arm. She starts in circles at her shoulder and under her armpit and slowly works down to her bicep, then triceps to her elbow, then her forearm to her wrist, and finally, her hand. With her thumb and forefinger, she delicately separates each knuckle, spreading equal amounts of lotion in between crevasses. She uses this method everywhere—wondering if she will be able to bend over far enough to reach it all. Focused on herself, Stella's no longer disgusted at stretch marks, cellulite, folds, and varicose veins. Her only thought is lavender. Completely coated and glistening, she goes back to her bed and lies down on top of the covers.

There are screeching sounds in the night that Stella cannot hear because she's purposefully turned up the volume on the bedside clock radio.

"Maybe they'll scratch his eyes out. Eat him. Or bury him." Stella blushes at the thought.

A spicy samba plays. She reaches between her mattress and box spring and retrieves the book she's secretly rescued from Frank and the raccoons earlier that night, *How to Spice Up Your Life in the Bedroom.*

Flea
for Samantha

Having no better flesh to fester, the flea burrowed
its way into my life. I'd come home greasy and
grimy as usual. Feeling dirty after finishing up
the day's accounts and writing my last letter to
some delinquent builder, knowing I'd cheated one
more inch of this muck heap of a world in doing
my boss' bidding. The wretch had hired me as a
secretary at first, something I swore I'd never be.
Despite my youthful and naïve efforts to become
an original, I accepted the job because I needed the
money. But after battling sex-role stereotypes along
the Mississippi and surviving the wrath of seven
generations of dumb men while liberating all of the
mothers in my family with nothing more than my
wanderlust, Canadian passport, and good hygiene,
I learned to put up with the boss' creeping and
leering eyes, his bad-breath jokes, and the smell of
his cheap aftershave. I even accepted the collection
of pubic hair that he'd left crawling on my desk:
gagged then, gagged now. He'd since promoted me

to his assistant. I was paid the same and still had to brew the prick his mud-dark coffee. It wasn't the actual work that I detested. But helping to sell off real estate in the form of shoebox condos for a price that could feed a village was gross. I resented my sellout most because I felt tarnished, tainted. I was unclean, and the whole thing stank, the way I did now coming home.

My hair was a kind of rat's nest chic. My cheeks, sweating. I guess I put up with the gig because the boss let me wear jeans as long as they were tight-fitting. Besides, I could spend most days laughing with my pal, Mina. She was the other secretary/assistant hired around the same time I was. I never understood why he needed two secretaries, but his wife said it was because we were both terribly attractive, athletic, and young, and we both liked to giggle. Four things that the poor old girl had lost somewhere in her battle to survive the degenerate she called her husband. God only knows how he tormented her, and the great pains she must have endured. I felt sorry for her when she first came by the office to check Mina and me out. I saw her in varying shades of grey because she always wore grey power suits and seemed to get skinnier with each visit. She was lost in dying fabric. A draped collection of bones. No matter how much makeup she would apply to her sinking face, she couldn't disguise her fade into the background of her own life. The nicer I'd be to her, the more like oatmeal she'd become. Bland. Tasteless. When I first met her, I thought I'd try to save her, the way I do with all sad luck stories. But as time went on, and my attempts at kindness were met with a vacuum of jealousy, I began to lose sympathy for the woman. After all, she had married the bog.

Still, it was precisely this loss of compassion in myself that bothered me. I was becoming uncaring. I was apathetic. When I looked in the mirror, I too began to see a kind of grey streak creep in, and it bugged me. Not that I spend much time thinking about it; I don't wear makeup and I won't colour my hair when it turns grey. And I'd always sworn I wouldn't be consumed by a weary haze of dissatisfaction or blurred by smoke clouds of tedium. Yet the stink on me didn't lie. It was real. The house reeked too.

I threw open the door to my bedroom to find my cat, Manley, had puked up his salmon pâté all over my marigold bedspread. I couldn't get angry at Manley because he was so old. I was actually glad he had attempted to eat something. I cleaned up the mess and joined him on the floor. When I bought him from a pawnshop owner a few years back, I knew he was going to be an interesting cat. I could only imagine the freak who had traded him in for a few dollars to pay the rent, and I wondered if he intended on ever coming back for him. Then, Manley had a shining, jet black coat with a touch of white in his face and throat. He was always content. I had stumbled into the pawnshop looking for antique board games and was drawn to Manley's incessant purring. I wanted to purr like that. I always liked the way laughter or singing felt. I could feel his vibrations as much as I could hear them. Recently though, Manley had become more carpet than music box, and it hurt. He lay there, unmoving. No rhythm. No sound. He saw me or sensed me because I was pretty sure he'd lost his vision and chortled a little. He opened up one eye and, in secret, continued to breathe.

I ran my long fingernails across his body. Tufts of graying fur came off him like dust clouds. He was always shedding now, no matter the season. Everyday I'd sweep up enough Manley to assemble three more pussycats. I thought about collecting the fur the way I did as a child. In fact, I started to. I kept it in a shoebox under my bed, but threw it away for fear that my roommates would find it and make fun of me. Before, I would never have cared what anyone thought about my oddities. Pulling out a couple of handfuls of Manley and holding them up to the light, I regretted giving up that collection. I lifted the cat up above my head. His body sagged, and his purring picked up until the pressure from my hands against his chest was too much for him, and he began a slow, dry heave. It rose up from his hind quarters. I set him down on the ground. Feebly, he arched his back and continued the mechanical act. He thrust forward through the length of his body towards his quivering mouth. I hated watching it, especially thinking that I'd caused it. But, just as the spasm grew too much for me to bear, it stopped with a crackling cough. The cat resumed his limp pose on the floor, unnerved, as if the only reason to ever rise was to heave. Sleep was a happy alternative. I longed for it myself.

And I would have fallen asleep right there on the hardwood floor. I tried, but a restlessness set in that had me writhing wildly. It wasn't the floorboards either. Although I was lying on a fine layer of strewn litter bits, I could sleep anywhere. It was one of my private talents—those hidden traits that only the individual who possesses them can appreciate. I could spell incredibly well. I could get people to confess to me their darkest secrets without asking. I could hold my breath for two full minutes. And, if I had to, I could sleep standing up. I'd been perfecting these routines since I was a kid. So, not being able to sleep, especially after a day of nonsense, drove me mad. It was like forgetting how to spell Mississippi. With the mounting frustration— another rarity, for one of my routines was sublimating all desire—I spiraled into a kind of frenzy which manifested into a scratching fit. An itching fit. It started off as a benign tickle, but soon grew into a fire crawling throughout my body. I scratched my arms red and raw up to my shoulders and neck, behind my ears and inside them too. My fingers moved across my body like a pianist's losing the battle with Shostakovich. When they settled on my scalp, I scratched at my skull until my brain bled.

I steadied up in the midst of the conniption, trying to locate the exact source of the itch. Trying to locate an itch usually makes me blush and feel vulgar. I centred myself and began a series of relaxation exercises that had been shown to me in college by my boyfriend. He was a video artist whom I had never seen lose his cool in all the weeks we dated. His exercises worked well. The problem was that I couldn't stand the bizarre videos that he made, or "birthed," as he liked to say. They made me feel stupid. The hand-held camerawork gave me headaches. The choppy editing made me puke. I was forced to use his New Age meditation techniques, which he took strange pleasure in teaching me, after each one of our dates. It was as if he knew the tremendous work and concentration involved in dating him and the anxiety he induced. Still, the exercises were something I was able to work into my life's repertoire. Lately, I had been turning to them more and more. The way I did now: standing with my feet apart, my back straight against the wall, face forward. I inserted my index finger into my belly button. I allowed another blushing moment of vulgarity to pass over me. I breathed in purple and breathed out yellow (the video artist's words, not mine). With precision, I began to spell words out loud: supercilious, aerodynamic, mortification, misogyny, anarchy, serotonin, Appalachian, disembowel. This spelling technique was not the video artist's. He mistrusted words. The idea was all mine. He disliked it. In fact, I think that was why we eventually split. Irregularity, dysfunctional, happenstance, formaldehyde. I savoured each letter on my lips and tried to picture them pour out of my mouth and turn into tiny butterflies.

It was working well until the middle of crustaceous when my spelling bee therapy got cut short. I spotted Manley acting strange.

He was standing erect on my chesterfield, staring at me with fire in his blind eyes. I'd never seen him this way before. He was completely transfixed, following invisible movements in the air, as if tracing the flow of letters from my mouth. His precision was exquisite and equally terrifying. It seemed to me that he was mirroring the invisible movements of my unravelling. The damn cat was in his pre-hunt. The prey: particles of my madness which I assumed only cats can see. Under the cat's eyes, a hateful growl grew. Manley had been reborn into a sphinx, and it scared the hell out of me. My scratching episode had somehow conjured the animal, and although I was glad to see him alert for the first time, I couldn't bear his stare. I bolted out of the room, down the hall, and landed safely inside the shower.

I hated taking showers and usually followed a specific schedule to offset the nuisance, but this impromptu session was justified because of the insufferable itch. I ran the water, engaged the faucet, and, standing directly under the stream, let the rush overtake me then. The lather routine was precise. In equal density, counting each revolution in my hands, I counted out loud as if numbering each chew of an undercooked pot roast before swallowing. I remembered my first shower. It was memorable because I had resisted it for so long. It wasn't the idea of getting clean that I minded, for I hate feeling dirty. It was the giving up of my baths. I didn't understand why I had to stop taking baths where I could not only do the job, but also play with ducks, boats, plastic fish, and a variety of other floating wonders, in order to stand at attention under a relentless assault. But it was put to me that it was part of the maturing process. I responded in protest by only showering with my clothes on. It was a story that my mother loved to retell at family gatherings or any time anyone on earth ever announced that they were going to have, or just had, a shower.

"Make sure you remember to take your clothes off."

And I hadn't undressed this time either. I realized this as I looked down at my clinging clothes that seemed pathetic to me— drenched, drowned. My blouse clung to me like wet curdling paint. My polka-dotted skirt was a tangled curtain that strangled my hips and legs. My knees protruded inappropriately—two pitiful bumps under the spotted soaking cloth. I'd done it on purpose, I tried to tell myself, just like those first few glorious rebel showers. I began to see the dye from my pink socks run streaks down the drain. Then all kinds of colour started bleeding from me. It was amazing. A liquefied rainbow spun circles around me as it made its way down. It seemed like such a waste of brilliance. The colour was being washed from me, taken from me, and I just stood there, obedient, and let it happen. I was prepared to stand there draining until the water ran clear, but I noticed something remarkable about my pruning hands. They'd been infused with a kind of peacock blue. I lifted my skirt to find purple ankles. Ripped off my socks from neon feet. I tore off all my clothes until I was nude and discarded them in a loud pile in that chamber. I shut off the water for fear that my new hue would be rubbed off.

Out of the shower and in the mirror: my body was a watercolour painting in violet, peach, and crimson. I explored my skin as if chancing upon some secret land formation at dawn. And the sun's playing with the moon, and the sky's changing the look of the land, and the water's not water, it's light. I'd never made it a routine to stare at myself naked, but these pictures of me were captivating. I immediately thought to store away the practice for the future. I would perfect the colours of my body with time.

I left pink footprints down the hall. My roommates would be furious, but I didn't care. I loved the look of them. To spite the white carpet further, I made unnecessary turns in the living room: walking in figure eights, inventing dance steps as if playing an endless, reckless game of hopscotch. I whirled around the place with pink abandon until my feet were bare and floated back into my bedroom.

The cat was back at it. He was in a frenzy, gnawing on himself. From the bulky, ancient, and decrepit body, a contortionist emerged. He burrowed his sharp teeth deep into his hollow. Without warning, he leapt spastically into the air, up and off all fours. I swear to God the cat was flying. He was bouncing and shrieking up and down and ricocheting off the walls. I wanted to see it as a kind of enchanted dance. I longed for him to be wearing some corny satin costume, but this was no act. He was killing the fucking flea that had tormented us for months.

"Kill it! Kill it! For Christ's sake!"

I was trembling, watching the hunt. I was still wet and dripping, my colours running off my freezing body. The cat snapped one last time in mid-air, and with it, his mania came to an abrupt end. He was suddenly still. I heard him purr deliberately. I saw him blinking at me as if adjusting his eyes to the brightness of my body. Then he wound down like a dying motor. Manley, like the flea, was dead. Catching it had been his final mission. It was more. It was what had kept him alive for so long. By the end, he'd only been living for the sole purpose of stopping the constant pestering.

I picked him up and held his body against mine. I wrapped him in one of my silk nightgowns and got dressed quickly. I felt like a moron and knew I'd have to clean up my mess before my roommates came home. But giving Manley a proper burial was my sole focus. The problem as I saw it was that there was no land that had any meaning for me here. Since coming to the city, I had lived in apartments or shared a backyard with strangers. No ground was sacred enough for me. If I had been back home, I would have buried the cat under my grandmother's porch. But my grandmother and her porch were long gone. They barely survived in my memory. For there are people and structures that once existed in my head that seem to disintegrate into sand with each year. The only spot I could think that might serve as an appropriate gravesite was a lot that my boss had just broken ground on. It was in the north end pocket of the city surrounded by woodlands. It was either that or take the cat back to the pawnshop.

I put Manley inside a duffle bag, put the bag in a basket at the front of my bicycle, and set off through the fall evening. It was beautiful to ride that way through the drift of solemn trees. Red and orange leaves rustled on our path. My approach was a kind of funeral procession. I didn't feel weighed down by the dead cat. I rode with a secret in my basket, and besides, I always feel like that when riding. We arrived as the sun was going down. No one was around. The site seemed so vacant now because of the absence of workers or construction. The lone billboard advertising the soon to be erected condos read: Dream away, if you dare. It made me spit up in my mouth. I wanted to set it on fire and watch it burn. I hoped Manley would haunt the building for years to come. I'd field tenant complaints about faulty heating and rattling windows knowing that it was his ghost stalking the halls.

There was a huge crater dug up, and I knew the foundation was set to be poured the next morning. On impulse, I crept to the edge of the hole on my bike and hurled myself down the steep incline. It was exhilarating. I made it safely to the bottom and started to dig. The ground was hard, but I managed. I dug on all fours, pushing the dirt behind me. It was a shallow grave, but it was the best I could do in the dying light. I placed the wrapped-up cat inside and completed my funeral game with a prayer. The words the cat was flying lingered for a moment on my lips.

The approach of a vehicle at the top of the hill cut my blessings short and muted me. Intense head lights shone across the wide expanse. I heard the crunching and flattening of stones. I was terrified to be found down there. I ditched the prayer and the bike and began my climb. My breathing became thick. I felt as though my gums were bleeding. An attack was coming on. I didn't want to be questioned by some asshole security guard or some no neck foreman, or worse, my degenerate boss. For I recognized his pimped out SUV when I made it to the top. It was idling close to the edge of the abyss. I wanted to disappear. Go back down and bury myself beside my cat. I thought I'd die if he saw me or found Manley. But surely he had already, for his vehicle had not budged at all during my ascent. I was standing in clear view. I decided to brace myself and face him instead of running away like a coward. What the hell was he doing there anyway? I reached the tinted window and stared inside. I could feel eyes on me, mocking.

The window lowered. The gaunt face of my boss' wife was scarlet. She wore a violent grin; her mouth, a kind of upturned gash. She was panting slowly.

"Isn't it lovely," she said. "I love watching the harvest sky when the sun goes down. Don't you, dear? Look."

And pointing out beyond the pit, I saw the enchanted playground of the sun and moon in a sudden vastness of space and colour.

"So beautiful," she continued to mutter in a voice as calm as the night. Although next to her, bound, gagged, and wrapped in garbage bags with duct tape, a man buzzed and writhed, wriggled and kicked on the passenger's side.

Funeral Polka

I found Papa naked and drunk, asleep in the tub. The low water level showed a good part of his belly above the lip of the bath. I reached down into the almost-ice between his ankles and pulled the plug on the all-night Papa soup. The gurgling of the drain and the splash from my hand woke him. The bath water emptied out. Papa came to. I grabbed a towel from the cabinet and offered it to him. He stood, trembling slightly, water dripping from his white body. Hunched. Extended. I wrapped the towel around the wet little man and urged him out. He grasped at my body and pressed his wet face against my chest. He told me he was glad I was home. I disentangled myself from his arms and pushed him out the door and down the hall to his room. His feet left prints on the rug. I picked up the bottle of homemade red wine he'd emptied and brought it to the kitchen.

    I was surprised to find the room was in impeccable condition: the dishes were clean, the floor had been swept, and the counters were clear. The only mess was a pile of newspapers and mail by the door. The living room too was immaculate—everything in order, in its right place. The dining room table was set the way Mama kept it on Sundays: the good china out beside two candles, beside decorative flowered napkins. Three places. Everything looked to have been polished down. I wasn't sure if the work had been done recently or had simply been left that way from when Mama last set it.

Papa scurried out in a blue housecoat—legs and feet bare. I busied myself by starting up some eggs for him on the stove. I asked him when the funeral was going to be and grated cheese over the sizzling eggs just the way the old man loved. He sat down at the table and sighed. I grabbed a plate and shovelled out breakfast. He started in about the hospital fees and the assholes at the bank and the talk I was used to hearing. The talk of family debts and the hopelessness of our situation. I told him I'd get my old job back at the restaurant and set the eggs down for him.

Papa got up and hurried out of the kitchen. He came back in carrying a modest blue and purple urn with a gold-plated trim. His eyes filled up with tears, and he cried out something about not having the money to bury Mama. He had taken care of it in his own way. He collapsed back down on the chair. Crying without sound, sniffling. Salty tears fell onto his plate of eggs. I sat down next to him and stared at the canister. Papa flinched as I tried to hold it. He held his breath then let out a cry, quivering. He asked me to forgive him for taking matters into his own hands. He looked directly at me and put his head down on the table—sobbed—the urn pressed to his chest. I asked him if it had already been taken care of and he only wept back at me.

I examined the urn, seeing it differently now, since it contained the remains of my mother. I got up and grabbed the frying pan off the stove, went to the sink and turned the hot water on. Papa raised the urn, stared at it, put it down and stared off. He began a rant about Mama being a saint…Maria his love…his sweet one…Maria his little one…his voice, lyrical. I turned off the water and put the pan away.

"My beautiful darling one…"

He put the urn down, wiped his eyes and turned to the eggs. He ate them slowly. I promised Papa I'd play him something on the accordion later and went to my old room in the basement.

It was exactly as I had left it a year ago. I spotted my huge squeezebox in the corner. I had grown into it from the age of three, only to be of age to abandon the bloody thing. I found the number to the restaurant and called my old employer. Nozar was sympathetic to my situation and offered his condolences as well as a fresh Middle Eastern perspective on death. He assured me that as long as he was cooking up pies, I'd have a job delivering them. I told him I'd need the day to get a vehicle together, thanked him, and hung up.

The Dodge wouldn't turn over. It hadn't been driven in months. All the tires were flat and the windows showed the tint of the seasons. I popped the hood. All fluids were down and I seriously doubted my chances at getting the beast up and running, but I accepted the project and worked on it with what tools I could find in the garage. (I removed the tranny.)

The Charlie Parker song that had haunted me for months all semester popped into my head. (I lubed her up.) It was a song that no amount of practicing or listening would help to get it inside my hands. I was unable to play it the way I heard it and the goddamn time signature and modal changes never made any sense—still didn't. (I went at the spark plugs with some WD-40.) It was the song that forced me to accept defeat as a saxophone player and piss away my time at college.

The sun beat down hard. I stared at it then looked away. I caught a glimpse of Papa through the upstairs window. He wore a hairnet and yellow gloves and was gingerly washing down the windows with a large sponge. When he spotted me, he disappeared. He ran out the front door a few moments later carrying a large bucket. I saw the rest of his getup: he still wore the housecoat, and now an apron tied around his waist. There were suds on his sleeves. He was thrilled to see me working on the car and began soaping it up. He worked intensely and continually muttered about how happy he was that I was home and how better everything was going to be now that I'd come back.

I tried to concentrate on my work. I wasn't up for any battles with Papa. Any guilt trips or going down memory lane to find Mama alive. I wanted to get the car going, make enough to settle things for him, and get the hell out of that town. But Papa's talk was relentless. He let me know that Mama got very sick by the end, but she never blamed me for leaving. He let me know that he never blamed me for leaving either and how he knew I'd come back to him. The truth was that besides Mama's death, my student loan had run out and I really didn't have much choice but to come home.

It was amazing to watch him work. I had never seen this

conviction in him before. Mama kept everything clean, and now that she was gone, maybe he wanted to honour her. His European obsession with cleanliness pushed his whole body against the car. He worked quickly and effectively. I heard a faint wheezing in his chest. He was somewhere else—in his head. As if he were not standing out there in his blue housecoat cleaning a shitbox. As if I were just a little boy working beside his dad. As if Mama were in the house cooking up tourtière or poutine or croque monsieur for us when we'd finished. As if we were living out the dream he had for us when he came to this country before I was born. As if Mama weren't just a handful of ash, but still the beautiful creature he'd always adored.

I could see the fresh, cool, morning spring air work on his skin. Ice formed on the body. It was too chilly out to be washing a car. I told Papa to leave it; that he'd get sick if he stayed outside the way he was dressed. He blew off my comments and worked away. He was a stubborn man. A simple man with an enormous heart. He couldn't be told anything he didn't want to accept. He'd reinvent, or dismiss, or deny. Just like he'd done with my taking off. He wouldn't take my rebellion, wouldn't let me hurt him. He was the eternal optimist, and did and thought what he had to so as to see things the way he wanted.

I forced the key. The engine sparked and rolled over. Papa was overjoyed. Papa was proud. He begged me to take him for a spin before I set out for work. I told him he could come along to get some gas and that satisfied him. We pulled away, out of that neighbourhood on the dead-end street in that dead-end factory town.

Inside the car, Papa kept up his cleaning: he sponged the dashboard, the mirrors, the radio. We passed by all the old haunts. My old high school, the mall, the church. Nothing had changed— why would it? When we passed by the graveyard, Papa became still, sullen. The old guy's heart was broken. He wouldn't forgive himself. He couldn't take heart in knowing he'd looked after her for all those years. The problem was that he didn't have the cash to bury her. I flicked on the radio. It was still set to his francophone station. A waltz played and seemed to soothe him a bit. I couldn't stand the piece.

We pulled into the gas station and I told him to stay in the car. I got out and pumped the gas. He rolled down the window and asked me to buy him a Pepsi-cola—he drank the stuff to help with indigestion. An upbeat polka played on the radio. I told him I would and went to pay. There were two ahead of me in the line. I grabbed a Pepsi. Glanced over at the car. Papa was squeegeeing the windows.

He was still in his housecoat and I could hear the music from inside. I paid.

A car of teenagers pulled up and took in the show. Papa was half-dancing as he worked, humming along and using the squeegee as a prop. I cringed and shot inside the car. The punks laughed. I started the engine. Papa jumped in. As we pulled away, he waved to his new friends. I rolled up the window and turned the music off. I gave Papa his Pepsi and he enjoyed it.

The restaurant was exactly as I remembered it. The smell of pizza and burning, the chaos of the back room, Nozar's sunshine girl pin-up collection. Nozar himself. I had never dreamed of going back to the place. I had devoted the good part of my high school years to it and knew it and loathed it. Nozar greeted me, gave me my first round of deliveries and I pressed on.

I tried to stave off the dread and uncertainty and failure that buzzed in my brain. How I'd gone directly back to the place I had tried so hard to flee. How all my ambition had been perverted. How now, I was in the same trap minus one. I kept the radio off and away from the jazz station to help with the denial of my bind. I couldn't turn towards dreams of freedom as I used to, because I didn't know what I wanted anymore. I ran away from my freedom. From school, from the saxophone, and from those pompous bastards in the city. I was back in the arms of my little father: Lou Garou.

I was ahead of schedule. I picked up twenty dollars in tips. I hated admitting I was a damn good delivery boy. Nozar gave me more pizzas, more addresses. I took a break at 11 p.m. Ate my complimentary slice. Daryl, another delivery boy, was anxious because he had been given the famous trailer park address of the woman who ordered pizza whenever her husband was away on business or in jail again. She was looking for a lay. Nozar usually went, but I guess he was busy that night. I had gone once years ago and would have lost my virginity to her, but my mind wouldn't accept it as any kind of romantic vision. I wished Daryl all the best. I delivered to ten more houses and went home.

Nozar always paid us under the table and I had eighty dollars to show for my efforts. I went looking for Papa. I was going to give everything over. I tried my parents' bedroom. The door was locked. I found it odd, because I didn't remember a lock on the door. Papa called to me from the bathroom. I went inside. He was in the tub again and held a fresh bottle of wine. The room was thick. I went to the toilet and urinated. I lay my earnings on the counter for him.

"You promised you'd play for me," he said.

He was a prune. He must have been soaking since I'd left in the morning. I looked at him naked in the tub. He looked like an ancient child. Lost. Soaking in his memories and sadness and stubborn ideals. I gave in. I went to the basement and lugged my accordion up the stairs. The case wouldn't fit through the bathroom door. I took out the instrument and brought it inside. I sat down on the edge of the tub and began.

I hadn't played in two years. I was surprised to feel that my hands and arms were awkward. Playing had always been second nature to me, but I was out of practice. I kept at it and squeezed out the polka. Forced my hands until I felt the years of playing at parties, at family gatherings, at birthdays and weddings and Christmas and recitals take over. Until the music poured out and there was nothing I could do to hold it back. Papa closed his eyes and surrendered.

I played for him and for Mama. I was a little boy again and cursing under my breath, biting my lip because I didn't want to play. But I did play. I played for hours. Everything I knew. Everything I'd been taught. And songs I'd never heard before. New songs. Coming to me from I don't know where. Everything pouring out of me and echoing full inside the tiled walls of that tiny bathroom. In that tiny little house—our home. I couldn't stop. No song was impossible, no idea beyond me or too much for me. I was playing for the dead.

Exhausted, I began to tremble. I couldn't hold onto it any longer. I let go and the accordion fell to the ground. I sat hunched over on the tub and cried. Papa looked up. We took in the sudden silence and let the ghostly polka music ring in our ears. He pulled himself up from the tub and walked out of the bathroom. I heard him call for me a few minutes later from inside his room. I used all my strength to stand up and walk out of the bathroom. I kept my head down and felt like an obedient son for the first time in my life. I pushed open the door. I went inside.

That's when I saw her. All in white. Lying on the bed. Her head resting on large pillows. Flowers everywhere in the room. Flowers pinned in her hair. A bed of flowers. Candles lit throughout the room. The window was open. A cool wind blew. Moonlight shone on her body. Mama. So still. So peaceful. So quiet. Gone. Papa sat on the edge of the bed and stared at her, his secret out. I went over and embraced him. Reached out and touched her forehead, soft, cold.

We worked together. Gathered up blankets. A Bible. Shovels. Flowers. We dressed for a cold night. Brought her body to the car. Drove out into the country until we found a place. Did what we could. Papa said a prayer. Papa—the little man with the huge heart.

"Maria, my lovely one, I love you."

We drove home after we finished burying Mama. Drove home together in that patched-up Dodge, exhausted. The sun was coming up on the nowhere town that I'd tried for so long to run away from. For the first time, I could see it—life. In dreams, and in my head, and in the nowhere town, or back in the city or back in that empty field or at the restaurant, or alone in a room somewhere, anywhere. And everywhere I saw it, and him too: Lou Garou, rebel father, Papa. With that damn accordion music playing all around us.

Tiny Miracles of
Moira Childs

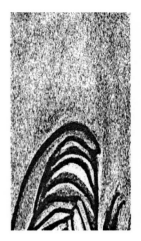

RESCUING JOHNNY

Hunched, slumped, enveloping his guitar with heavy arms wrapped around the mahogany body, he brings it close to his own. A stranglehold on the strained, strung neck, fighting to finger an F-sharp chord, but deformed—it rings out all wrong. Strumming like the tortured flick of a lion's tail on fire, his hair moving in tangles of sweat across his face, away and back again, he sways, conducting the nausea. It is his way of composing a *hurtin'* tune. But as the pictures in his head grow too grim to keep still, they spill out of flaring nostrils and the ringing holes of his ears.

It is clear to him that he'll soon lose the battle over melody: failing phrasing, key and rhythm— not enough, or too much, to convey the *Botched Affair*. And since despair is better served in a minor key anyway, he loosens his grip on the hook. This time, sly and steady, he strokes. He molests the axe, pawing the strings, the open belly of a cat. And

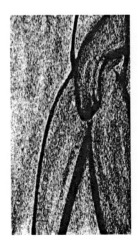

suddenly from somewhere inside him, a scratch of voice surfaces: turpentine, high-pitched, but quiet, made more from behind his eyes—nasal—than from his diaphragm or throat. All insect tone and perilous, drifting on the note.

He stares into the mouth of the guitar, hoping to find a new depth to darkness, a full-lipped kiss from an indifferent mistress. But the void only stares straight back. The circle and its hollow seem hungry. Yes, enough to devour that hand if it comes too close. As it does, he loses his pick in a swallow, and the music stops.

Shaking the instrument now above his head, it rattles like a baby's angry toy. The tantrum echoes the agony of control. The hole is a drain and he plunges down deep, snaps the tight high E-string, the B and the G, goes in sore to the middle of his forearm. He gropes in the dark, feeling his way around cobwebs and splinters. He'll rip its goddamn head from its goddamn neck, and rip its goddamn neck from its unholy body, if it comes down to that.

But the hole fights back: something bites his wandering pinkie finger. He withdraws his hand, shoots it straight into surrender and lets out a scream, a high C. I scamper into the room then and find my big brother, wide-eyed and sucking, tending to the attack, jilted, with slobber on his sleeve. I retrieve the guitar from the floor and peek inside with sideways surprise and curiosity, and reaching in I pull out my white pet mouse by its tail. It dangles upside down, willful and deaf, with the guitarist's pick between its razor-sharp teeth.

SAVING LEWIS

After supper, bloated, with his face turning as red as Shiraz, he asked me to bring warm milk to the study where he stretched out on the sofa with Shostakovich. Surrounded by books, some his own publications, he ran a wild sweat. In the hall, with a trembling, birdlike, awkward stalk, I appeared with a mug in my hands that seemed to hold sway over my small frame. I tiptoed in, not wanting to disturb him, but got caught up on the rug and fell, launching the milk across the room. It crashed and rained down on a pile of his notes on a desk by the window. I gasped, rushed to the mess, and began to whine apologies, mopping it up with the hem of my skirt—a frenzy born out of real memories of my father's stormy temper, but the man remained motionless, though his skin seemed to crawl with a constant flow of perspiration.

The silence scared me even more. I was sobbing, dull, and wet from sopping. Did it occur to him: *dismiss her or console her*? But instead, he stewed in his man-made puddle, watching tears form and fall from my face, listening to the intermittent keening, interrupted by a quivering diaphragm. In his mind first, but then in his gut, he started to mimic my spastic breaths until he just had to laugh outright: a chuckle, until it was uncontrolled. The outburst startled me. And although suspect, I now laughed along with Dad. He motioned for me to come to him and I did—bounded towards him, jumped into his arms, sprawled on top of his giant, shuddering belly.

The two of us stayed that way—wet, pressed, and goofy—until it was clear that he was no longer laughing at all, but choking and heaving, sitting up slippery as a fish, seized by the fit. I reeled to my feet, took aim at the back of the leaping sea monster and drove in tiny fists. His body resounded, loud and hollow as a drum. My rhythm was exquisite and savage. I climbed on top of his chest and sat down. I grabbed his huge head in my hands and, with his mouth a gaping hole, peered inside past his purple tongue. I reached in up to my wrist, struggled, and grabbed it—an intact piece of writing paper. Soaked through, blood red, and crumpled, I regarded it with wonder. But he was not surprised at all to see the damned thing, just grateful that he could breathe once again.

WAKING CONSTANCE

Overtaking the shore and Constance, the tide—hypnotic—swept in on time and claimed her sketchbook on the waves. The charcoal drawings blurred now, though the skeleton remained in a haze of grey. On doctor's orders, she'd come to sit and meditate and purge, but sleep covered her up like a blanket. When Constance awoke with the trickle of cold on her toes and the rattle of pebbles beneath, her teeth felt loose against her tongue and, flicking at the film in her mouth, she wondered if she'd swallowed a fish, more than a taste of the salty sun. In her eyes: sockets buried, blinded in seaweed-green and sand. The night had passed, starry and wet, like a painting in blue and yellow. She sat up fighting rust and the crick in her neck. Her pruned and wrinkled skin obeying her movements, Constance looked to the ocean, despite her ravaged vision, and saw a speck, a trembling boat. Helpless. The vessel, nauseous and drunk, was sinking like an abandoned toy as a lone, reckless silhouette fought a drooping sail. She waded out, desperate, but there was no mercy in the pantomime. She watched, submerged up to her waist, a current pushing through, surrounded by her floating sketches. The boat rang a feeble bell as it went under, and Constance barely registered the sound before it was silenced by the waves. She drifted back, grateful only for the morning bath that had cleansed her body and began, aimlessly, to walk away.

A rush of gulls—all wings and squawking music—lifted up and passed her, an ordered mania that replaced her own. Beneath their flight, Constance saw what she took to be her daughter dancing, her pale arms outstretched, directing the flock. I was flapping in mirrored joy and provocation, guarding a sandcastle that I'd built. Constance moved towards my beckoning as if in surrender. I stopped and stared at her for a moment, my eyes adjusting from the brightness of wings. I smiled and took Constance's hand and led her towards the battlements I'd shaped on the sand. Constance sat down and watched me carve with architectural precision. Then I reached up and extracted a small seashell from Constance's ear, and from that shell, miraculous, though cracked, I caught a perfect, hidden pearl. The find, a knowing delight, for I already had a place waiting for the treasure in the secret tower of sand. Constance remained transfixed, until I returned the shell and held it to her ear and listening to the hum inside it, Constance said she heard the lingering seashell sound of another child's sea-lost voice in her awakening.

ANOINTING FLORENCE

Barely able to bend her aged body, she assumes the child's pose and presses her knees down into supple earth. The garden's birth encourages her to work with razor-sharp exactitude. The attitude is natural, though her hands sometimes shake. They are leather and chapped but balance her weight well enough as she prunes. Overwhelmed by the smell coming off the begonias, irises, and sunflowers, she tilts her head back and away from the gaping bed, but is blinded by a tyrannical sun. Now all she sees is spotted by swelling black dots that swarm and devour her breathing Van Goghs.

She rises and she rises and she rises with a rose, dizzy, everything in threes, she tramples all the pansies beneath her clumsy, oversized, black-and-yellow rubber rain boots. It's more than a kiss from the sun: she's being stung by a gang of angry bees, whose nest shrieks once discovered. She fights back and swats fiercely, arms flailing against the piercing pinches of warm flesh. They stick her face with tiny tails, her hands, her wrists. Stick her forearm and right ankle. Stick the fat part of the arm and behind the right ear. Crawl underneath her clothes and buzz: sting her back, her belly, her chest. Sting her forehead, her elbow, her nape. She leaps into a patch of overgrown grass and drops to her knees and rolls among the weeds. Her voice is a crackle of pleas, but they stick her on her stinging tongue, too, and it begins to bulge like blubber until it is too fat to fit inside her mouth. Silenced, she forces her eyes closed and listens for the buzzing to stop. They quiver, caught inside the folds of her skin and continue to hum as they die, droning on and on. I find my grandmother curled up on the ground and begin to pluck out the stingers that jut from her body. Tiny hands pull over thirty pins from the old woman—a seething, pink pattern developing close to the soil. I pick up her tin watering can and tip it, sprinkling water over all I see of her flowering sores.

Matadors in Pink

On the flatbed pickup truck—belching up gas, kicking up dust clouds, bouncing through the grounds of the mansion's estate—I was desperate and holding onto rattling stacks of pre-made hors d'oeuvres and clanging bottles of wine. My tuxedo shirt was sweating blood. I was prepared to impale the driver with my corkscrew, with its stainless steel curves that were reflecting a sharp glint of moonlight.

"Whoa!" As if calling to a horse, he turned his thick head towards me, revealing buckteeth, then spit a wad through the open window. I sustained his driving stare. Ravaging our way through the bush, I started to doubt the existence of the house, but after a final climb, fly, and landing, Bucky pulled up. It was a colossal place in deep reds and yellows. I heard flamenco music, and the sound of laughter and clapping. I started collecting my gear, but Bucky told me to leave it and go inside. I left him wheezing with the load.

I approached the front door and knocked. My

knuckles peeled off wet red paint. I wanted it off me immediately and bent down and dragged my hand against the grass. Bucky brayed at me to show myself in. He was now sitting cross-legged on the flatbed, stuffing his fat face with pâté. He licked the stuff off his stubby fingers and washed it down with red wine. Between swallows: gasps. I showed myself in.

The flamenco music echoed through the impressive entrance way. The vaulted ceiling was awe-inspiring, though I could only just glimpse the grandeur of the architecture because of the low light. Massive, gaudy candles flickered throughout the house. There were voices at the end of the hall, all falsetto. I followed the high-pitched sounds, wondering where the hell I was. I had only taken on the gig because I was flat broke, again. I hadn't landed a commercial in two years, ever since I started packing on weight. Bartending paid the bills, and usually allowed me to memorize lines. I had a copy of the play *The Zoo Story* in my back pocket. I needed to finish memorizing a speech for an early morning audition. My character, Jerry, tells how he attempts to kill a dog.

From out of the party room at the end of the hall came a masked man scurrying on all fours. The mask was studded with jewels, and he was clad in violent pink satin, a matador's outfit. He was the source of the squealing, and he continued to let the sour note soar. I heard his knobby knees, like trotters, knocking against the wooden floor. He was a bag of bones in costume. He made a beeline in my direction, but stopped inches away from my feet. Suddenly mechanical, he jerked his head up towards me. A white shock of beard sprouted out from under his hidden face. I tried to introduce myself, but he hushed me, bringing a long bony finger to his mouth hole. With great pains, he tried to stand. I offered him my hand on instinct; it was still smeared in red. He took my hand in his and managed to make it to his feet where he stood hunched like a human question mark. I could see he was ancient. His weary stance was a sharp contrast to the manic crawl I'd just witnessed.

"They mustn't see your face," he whispered. "Where the hell is your mask?"

Before I could answer, he ushered me down the hallway into a room lit with green light.

"Everything must be perfect," he said. "It's my birthday for Christ's sake!"

The walls of the room were adorned with artefacts: swords,

intricate metals, animal heads, peacock feathers, and masks. There were also statues of figures with huge pricks everywhere. One phallus was three times the size of the beholder. I couldn't help but laugh. The old man turned on me with a razor hiss.

"You find this funny? You think showing up to my birthday without a mask is a joke?"

I silenced myself. The old guy was muttering under his hot breath, fussing with a moveable staircase on wheels. He wheeled the contraption across the room. The pitch of rubbing metal mimicked the whinge of his throat. He positioned the staircase and started to climb. At the top, he clutched two masks under his right arm and continued to mutter, flustered. He turned around on the stair and glared down at me. His pointy boots were at the level of my head.

"Matador, or bull?" he asked.

"Excuse me?"

"I already have! Matador, or bull?"

"I don't understand the question."

"Bloody hell!" He stomped his feet. "Are you a matador, or are you a bull?"

As he frantically repeated the two options, he thrust his pelvis back and forth for matador, and then curled his shoulders up to his ears in surrender for bull.

"Matador, or bull?"

In his hysteria, he lost his footing and fell. His scream on the way down sounded like a flock of dying gulls. I snatched the old geezer out of the air. He was weightless in my arms, and still clung to both masks. I held him like a child, and he was thrilled.

"You saved me! Oh my arse! You have saved me on my birthday!" In my grip, he returned to his former singsong self. The one I had first met, squealing on all fours.

"You are strong, you go both ways, both matador and bull. I was leaning towards bull, but now I feel that matador is more appropriate. Matador, like me."

I put him down and he handed me the mask.

"Put it on!" he ordered. I did. "Exquisite! Now give it a minute before you join us." On his hands and knees, he took a deep breath and scurried out of the room, back down the hall, shouting, "Ole!"

I took a picture on my phone of the jumbo cock statue to send to my ex-girlfriend, counted to sixty, and followed after the matador in pink.

The party room was painted in muted terracotta and lit with candles in freestanding holders. An entire group appeared before me. Like the pink matador, they were all ancient and hysterical, all masked, all dressed in brilliantly coloured satin. In all my years on stage, I'd never worn anything as beautiful as what these men had on. In the corner of the room, I found the source of the flamenco music. A very tall, thin, black-haired, masked musician strangled a Spanish guitar.

I found my bar. There were no signs of Bucky, so I decided to start to work without the product that the catering company had sent with me. It was a tight spot, but I was used to serving drinks in various settings. This one was proving to be the most bizarre, but once I had everything set up, I relaxed.

No one was drinking. The men were lost in their multicoloured satin dance moves. The guitarist in the corner was lost inside his playing technique. I leaned on the back of the bar and pulled out *The Zoo Story*. The room was loud, but I still managed to go over my lines. The difficulty of my speech was remembering all the details of the attempted killing. My character decides to kill the dog, devises a plan, puts rat poison in hamburger meat, and then gets the dog to eat the meat. I was stumbling on the section dealing with remorse for trying to kill the dog. I didn't quite know how to play it: victim turned victor turned victim again. It was tough. I was getting soft. I felt that I'd been losing my acting chops the more I worked as a bartender.

The smell of burning oil made me nearly puke in my mouth. The room filled with smoke. There was a dazzling hookah pipe by the window, and the old guys were blowing hard. As the smoke rose up in the room, I noticed a new step to their dance. It was no longer wild and flaying, but severe and uniform. The group formed a circle when the music stopped and the host, that strange old matador in pink, entered the circle.

"It's my birthday!" The group bellowed and applauded. "It's my birthday and I love you." More bellows and applause. "But no one here loves me." There was a ruckus response to the pink matador's words. "It's true! I am one of the unloved. I am ninety years old and nobody loves me."

I could see that he was playing at some kind of sick game, but I couldn't begin to know where it was going.

"If you love me . . . you'd kill for me!"

At this moment, the group broke off into pairs. The ancient

masked men began slapping one another across the face. They didn't
fight; rather, they traded smacks. The matador in pink responded to
each belt across the face with a glorious squeal and a corresponding
stomp of his boot heel. I could tell that they had done this before: it
seemed rehearsed, played out countless times. They were beating one
another.

"You do love me, you do, you do, you do!" The pink matador
was beside himself.

I tried to get the attention of the musician, but he had collapsed
in the corner, propped against the wall, his legs folded out before him
like those of a dead praying mantis.

There was a sudden commotion in the centre of the room. A
portly man in green was lying on his back, clutching his left arm. I
jumped the bar and ran to him. All of them seemed bothered by my
intrusion. I felt them breathing on me. I knelt down to tend to the
man in distress. I began by trying to remove his mask.

"Don't you dare remove that mask," ordered the matador in
pink. "Remove this sorry tub of guts, but don't you remove his mask.
It is clear that he does not love me."

The guitarist, resurrected, slashed the silence with a chord. The
pack of ancient revellers resumed their floggings.

I helped the man to his feet and ushered him into the hallway.
Sat him down on a large, high-backed leather chair, and pulled off
his mask. He wasn't conscious, but was still breathing. Sweat poured
down his round cheeks, and his face was red and puffy. Seeing him up-
close and distorted, I almost didn't recognize him. It was my acting
professor from university. Needing a minute to think of what to say
if he came to, I went back to my bar to get some ice. I was torn. That
bloated green man had always been a cruel bastard to me in school.
He used to try to get into our heads. He would make us cry, make us
relive disturbing memories. He was always after me about my weight.
I didn't want to help him, but decided I would. By the time I made
it back to where I'd left him in the hall though, he was gone. All that
remained was his mask and a pool of sweat from his satin ass.

I was rattled as I made my way back to the party. If I left now, I
wouldn't be paid. The group had finished slapping each other and had
settled into a more mellow mood, stumbling around and mirroring the
movements of the matador in pink. It reminded me of some of the
idiotic drama games I was forced to play in class. For the life of me I
couldn't understand how "pretending to be wind" would make me a

better actor.

"Dog!" shouted the pink matador. Instantly, the pack of ancients dropped down on all fours and began mimicking the actions of dogs, mostly smelling the other dogs' privates.

"Lion!" roared the pink matador, and the group followed his command.

"Peacock!" The men rose and began to strut. They extended their chests, spread their arms, and moved around the room with long strides.

"Bull!" I watched the peacocks morph into snorting, broad-backed bulls. But this act was different. Instead of puffing and prancing about, the bulls turned towards me at the bar. "Now we come to our main event. Everybody loves a good bullfight on their birthday!"

I could see their beady, bloodshot eyes piercing through their masks, trying to penetrate me. The praying mantis in the corner found his strength and played with fire. I bolted, jumped the bar, and ran down the hall. The bulls snorted after me.

"We are matadors, you and I!" the pink matador yelled. "Come back, coward. It's my birthday. I want a bullfight for my birthday!"

I managed to make it to the door, and I realized that if need be, I could outrun the old men. I almost started to laugh at myself as I opened the front door and ran directly into Bucky's barrel chest. He reeked of goose liver and vinegar. Pissed, he was wearing a bull's mask. Bucky grabbed me by the hair and threw me back. I landed in a patch of begonias in the front yard. One by one, the ancients stumbled out and formed a circle around Bucky and me. The pink matador appeared at a second-storey balcony.

"Ole!" he screamed.

I pulled off my apron and gave those old bastards a show. Bucky lunged, I dodged. Bucky countered, I sidestepped. With every charge from Bucky, I was able to get out of the way. I felt completely connected to my body. Rooted. My breathing was deep from my diaphragm; I was giving the performance of my life. As Bucky snorted his way at me, I could taste his hot breath at the back of my mouth. I took out my corkscrew and stuck him in the gut. The bull collapsed in a heap at my feet.

The men grew silent, I felt as though I could hear their bones shifting. I looked up at the matador in pink on his balcony. He was weeping profusely on his birthday, throwing down violent pink roses on the makeshift bullfighting ring. The men picked up the roses and stared down at their feet, their bodies sagging in the moonlight as they, too, all started to weep. I went over to tend to Bucky. I managed to get him to his feet and hand him a bottle of wine from the truck. Bucky took a swig and passed the bottle to me. When we were able to catch up with our breathing, Bucky and I also wept big fat tears. Pink roses continued to fall.

Francis and the Animals

Everything is different now. The pulse of the city, the way it looks, the way people look now; the cars they drive and their hairstyles; the clutter of the city, and its noise, and its fast pace, and its paranoia. I don't fit. I keep my head down as I move and try not to stare at the most common things, like street signs and the signs in storefront windows, the width of the sidewalks and the too-tame dogs that walk so leisurely beside uninterested owners; and mailboxes, and manhole covers, and bicycles chained up to posts, and the traffic's order, and almost every expression on every face I pass. I can't help but stare. Eyes fixed. Searching. Staring. At the women, too. Their bodies and movements and mouths. And the men they walk with, and the women they walk with, and the ones walking alone. I've been out for an hour now.

From out of my coat pocket, I pull the address to the halfway house: 181 Beaumont Avenue. I'm on the street. See the place—181. A tenement-style hotel co-op, five floors, red brick, faded white

windowpanes, faded white broken-down fire escapes on either side. I go in.

A fat woman with short black hair is laughing with a worker-type just left of the front desk. She has large breasts. Her whole body laughs as she speaks in a loud, attacking voice.

"You're bad, Leo," she says. "No way."

With an arm on Leo's shoulder, she pushes him away and holds herself up at the same time. Leo laughs and tries to hold up under the pressure of the woman. They disappear out a side door, laughing, losing their balance.

I go to the front desk. There are four shelves in behind. Two dozen cubbyholes stuffed with papers, envelopes, packages, various things. Next to the shelves, there are rows of keys on hooks. A sign reads: "Welcome to the Beaumont." I see no one. Five minutes pass.

I'm staring off into a painting of a forest on the wall. No one comes. Another five minutes pass. A gangly man approaches from somewhere. He's eating an apple.

"Looking for a room?" he asks. "You shoulda rang the bell."

I don't respond.

"How long do you need it for?" He flicks on a computer. "We have daily, weekly, and monthly rates. And it's ten percent discount for seniors, if that applies."

"I'm Francis," I say. "Officer Bates sent me."

"Oh, right," he says, "I'm Manny."

"I'm Francis Logan."

He knows who I am. Probably has a file on me somewhere. My history. My record. My life. Manny reaches into a cubbyhole on the bottom shelf and retrieves a folder. Inside, I see pictures of myself as a young man. Straight on. In profile. Scared face. Lost. Lovesick.

"You're gonna be in room number seven, on the third floor, northwest side of the building, facing the street. And you'll share the second kitchen on the floor and share the main bathroom, but you'll have your own room. A bed, some sheets, a TV. No, sorry, no TV. I forgot there's no TV in that room, or maybe there is. I can't remember, anyway."

He reaches back and grabs a key.

"Don't lose it, and don't make copies!" he says. He hands me the key. I follow him down a hall to a staircase, then up the stairs.

"How long were you in for?" he asks.

I tell him: "Twenty years."

He can't believe it. Neither can I.

"Here you go, old man. You're home. If you need anything, you know what to do and where to find me."

But I don't. I don't know how to do anything. I don't know where to find anything, or anybody. I open up the door to my new cell and go inside. The carpet is brown and thin. The four walls are yellow, nearly white, and there is very little light in the room. When I put my suitcase down on the bed, the iron-spring mattress rattles. I look out the window to see that I'm across from a laundromat, a liquor store, a tiny grocery store, and what looks like an identical building to the one I'm in—The Gladstone. From out of a window, I see a man with a beard in a white undershirt leaning out of the top floor and looking down at the street. He seems bored, self-involved. He's smoking a cigarette.

I take in my room. There is a TV, a brown dresser with four drawers, a bed, a door to a closet, a dark red radiator under the window, a brown wooden desk with a phone and a burned-out lamp on it. The smell of must and old cigarettes is everywhere. My old room was half the size of this one. But this one doesn't have cement walls or bars. Also, now I carry a key.

I unpack my suitcase. I have very little: a pair of pants, socks, underwear, three white t-shirts, two dress shirts. I put all the clothes in the dresser and put my coat on a nail in the closet. The probation board has given me a package. I sit down on the bed and open it. There's a letter.

Dear Mr. Logan:
Please find enclosed a map of the city with a guide to the bus service. As per your request of finding you a job whereby there is limited contact with people, we were able to obtain for you an entry-level grounds keeping position at the zoo. We feel that the job will help you establish yourself as a mobile civilian. It pays ten dollars an hour. Please report for orientation and your first shift on Monday, April 2. You are reminded that your parole restricts you from leaving the province for one year. Officer Charlie Bates has been assigned to you as your parole officer. He will visit you at your new residence (181 Beaumont) every other Tuesday to monitor your progress. Direct any problems, questions, or concerns to

him. Good luck.

I look through the rest of the package, find a map, a Metro Zoo employee handbook, and a plastic card folder. In the folder, I also find a social insurance card, a health card, a probationary library card, a bank card, a zoo employee card with a picture of an elephant on it, and photo identification: SIN #623 341 959, OHIP #36788221, Library Member #8467, Bank Account #24058, Zoo #365.

I look at my photo ID. I look old and scared.

The last item in the package is a handmade card with a drawing of a large, deformed bird on the front. The bird looks most like an owl and has large, deformed genitals and blue and yellow wings. It's drawn and written in crayon and reads: "Hey, Saint Francis, you're free. Hope you get laid right away! Good luck on the outside from Buck and the boys in Cell Block D."

I place the card on the ruined, brown dresser and put the package in the top drawer—the deed to my freedom.

The one-hundred-dollar cash advance they've given me is burning a hole in my pocket. I put on my coat and leave the room. Down and out of the Beaumont hotel. I don't see Manny at the desk.

* * *

It's 4:30. I haven't eaten all day. Too nervous. Earlier, I passed on lunch with Bates and don't feel the hunger until now. A pain pierces my side as I cross the street and go inside the grocery store. There're no other customers around. Good. I walk up and down the aisles and don't know exactly what I want. It's strange to have such choice. I grab a loaf of sliced white bread, put it back, and grab a loaf of rye. Some bologna, some peanut butter, a chocolate cake, a jar of pickles, a jar of beets, a toothbrush, toothpaste. I stack each item on top of the others and curse under my breath almost dropping the stuff. A woman's voice comes from behind me, soft.

"Careful, sir," she says. "Let me help you."

It's the voice of a girl with auburn hair. She's wearing a blue apron.

"You're gonna lose it," she says and starts removing some of the stuff from my arms. I tremble slightly as her hand touches me. I stare at her face, then look away.

"You ought to use a cart," she says. "It'd be easier."

I feel weak. Too fucking beautiful. She places the items down at the checkout counter. I do the same with the ones I'm carrying.

"Can I get you anything else?" she asks.

Where do I begin? What can I say? I shake my head no. She rings in the food. Looking past her, I see a wall of cigarettes and tremble again. So much choice. She sees me staring.

"Are you sure you don't need anything else? A pack of cigarettes?"

I smile, relieved.

"What kind would you like?"

"Anything is fine," I say.

I feel my face go flush. Feel my hands sweat. My knuckles turn white. Feel my brain bleed. She searches, retrieves a pack and grabs a book of matches.

"Popular brand, I think," she says.

I want out of the store. I'm paralyzed. I pay the girl, grab the bags, and am gone.

I breathe clear outside and walk over to the liquor store. A dog sits tied to a post. He's sleek, short-haired, jet black, and doesn't seem uneasy at all. As I walk by, he sniffs my ass. Inside the store, the air is cool and clean. All the booze, chilled and sparkling and beautiful. Alcohol always flows inside prison, but only ever warm, cheap, and bootleg. I'm sick of it—sick of the gut rot. And it's never enough to do any real numbing. The guy stacking the booze is thin and sickly. He's wearing cowboy boots. I'm sold on a six-pack and a bottle of vodka for now, but I'll be back. I live so close. A free man.

I pay and leave. I cross the street. I walk up to the third floor and find my room. There's noise coming from inside. The TV is on. I push open the door. A fat man with a red hat is sitting on the bed smoking a cigarette in his underwear.

"Sorry, man, wrong room," I say, closing the door.

"No wait, Francis," he says.

I walk inside.

"Larry, Larry Gossford. Remember?"

I don't.

"You remember me from *The Don*, '94. I was a friend of Louis Rutherford. Leaky Larry—Leak the Freak, c'mon, man."

He sits on the edge of the bed—animated—his belly fully extended over his shorts.

My memory kicks in.

"Right, Larry, I remember," I say. I put the groceries and drinks down on the desk. We shake hands.

"I live one floor up, room twelve. I been here three years. I check out all the ex-cons who come in. There's about fifteen of us. But when Manny told me Francis Logan was coming, I thought, 'Shit, I know that son-of-a-bitch.' How are you?"

"Good," I say. "You?"

"So, so. I'm working as a janitor at this dive about three blocks from here—the Red Rooster. I don't complain. Where'd they put you at?" he asks.

"I don't know, fucking zoo, I guess."

"Yeah, well it feels good, eh?"

"What?"

"Being out."

"Right, yeah, for sure."

"You got any connections?" he asks.

"No." And I don't. None that I know of. That I can remember. That would remember me. My parents are dead. No brothers. No sisters. Everyone I know is either dead or in jail or forgotten. Like Larry.

"Shoot, man, don't worry," he says. "I can introduce you to people. Even some nice women if you like."

Larry sticks his white tongue out. I look at him straight.

"Sure can," he says. "I know some real nice ones."

"Oh yeah?"

"Hell, man, you must be aching."

Larry seems so relaxed, so well adjusted with life outside prison.

"Forget it," I tell him.

"No way."

He gets up and goes to the phone.

"What are you doing?" I ask. I feel my adrenaline like acid in my veins.

"I told you I know some real nice ones."

"Forget it, I just got out, I don't want to get busted."

"It's fine. I know the girl." He starts dialling. "She's my cousin, man."

"I don't have money," I tell him, and he puts the phone back on the hook.

"Nothing?"

"I had to buy food and that."

"Forget it. I'll put it on her tab."

He picks the phone back up and dials again, determined.

"Hey…hellooo! It's Larry. Hey, sweetheart. Put Veronica on."

My heart starts up. I get up and start putting the groceries into the dresser. I grab the vodka, open it, and take a long drink. It explodes in my mouth.

"Hey, it's Larry, what's going on…nothing. Look, I need a favour…his name is Francis."

I take another long drink, put the bottle down, and take off my coat.

"What? A friend, a friend of mine. What time do you get off tonight…perfect…my place, yeah, yeah, okay, see ya."

He hangs up the phone and smiles.

"It's on. You're really gonna like her."

I don't respond. I open up the bag of bread and package of bologna and start up a sandwich.

"You want one?" I ask.

"Naw, but I'll take a beer."

I toss him one. He catches it, opens it, and drinks.

"She'll be here after she gets off work, around eleven."

Larry lies back down on the bed with his beer. He seems pleased with himself, as if he's done a public service or donated to some kind of charity.

I close up the sandwich and open the jar of pickles—I don't have any forks, or plates.

"Go grab some things from the kitchen," Larry says. "There's plates and stuff. You can claim what you like. Nobody cares."

I leave the room and go down the hall to the kitchen. It's more of an alcove than an actual room. There's a stove, a refrigerator, an enormous microwave, and a sink. Above the sink is a cupboard—I find two plates, a few forks, and a mug. I put the dishes in the sink and run the water. I head back to my room. As I pass by, a door opens slightly and is quickly shut. I'm back in my room now. Larry has a new beer.

"People don't care about sharing things around here," he says. "Maybe I will take a sandwich, if that's okay."

I give it to him.

"Pickle?" I ask.

"Please," he replies.

I start to work on another sandwich. Larry downs his beer, gets up, and grabs another. The TV has been on the whole time. He flips the channels. Each image is fuzzy. He bangs on the set.

"Shitbox," he says. "Why bother?"

He turns it off and lies back down on the bed.

"So tell me, when will you be ready to get back in the game?"

His voice is direct and full of intrigue, as if he's been holding this question back from the beginning. I close up my sandwich and take a bite.

"I'm through," I tell him.

"No, that's just the parole board talking."

He thrives.

"I'm done with it." My voice is calm.

"Well, you'll learn fast that you may be done with it, but it might not be done with you."

Larry goes through his beer, gets up, and gets a fourth.

"I'm an old man, Larry," I say and munch my pickle.

"So you're just gonna live the rest of your days cleaning zoo," Larry yells. He's drunk. "I'm just saying, when, when you get bored of that, I got some connections. I got my fingers in a few hot pies."

He probably has a cut in a small prostitution ring (maybe a family business), a few lowball bets here and there, and most likely some junk on the side.

"Suit yourself, but you gotta be careful you don't crack." He speaks freely and balances the beer on his chest. "You been in a long time, a hell of a long time. It's gonna take some getting used to."

I finish my sandwich and open one of the two remaining beers. I give the other to Larry. We drink in silence. Larry is stretched out on the bed. I stare at his heaving gut, and lean up against the closet door. We finish our drinks. I collect the cans and put them in an empty grocery bag, pile the dishes on the cabinet, and put the food back into a drawer. My shirts are in the bottom, my undies and socks in the top, and the food is in the other two.

"Want some cake?" I ask.

"Cake? Oh no, no, I couldn't."

He's pissed himself. The icing on the cake is melting. I'm tired. We remain motionless in silence for another twenty minutes.

"I better go," he says.

My mind kicks in.

"What's gonna happen tonight?" I ask.

"What?" He sits up and holds his head. "What about tonight?"

"The girl?" I keep my head and voice down. "Veronica?"

Larry stands up and staggers around, then lets out a loud burp.

"Sorry, bro," he says. "That's the bologna talking."

He lets out a laugh and then implodes a little.

"Is she really coming here?" I can't hide the dread. Larry stares at me, puzzled.

"Yes! Sorry, yes, that's right at ten, after work." He walks over to the door and opens it. "I'm gonna honk, Franc." He goes out the door.

"I thought you said eleven?"

"Right, eleven, eleven, I'll send her down, man."

He bounces down the hall and out through a door at the end of the hall. I hear him coughing as he climbs the stairs to the upper floor.

She probably won't come. I can see how Larry has adjusted so well to living on the outside. Very little has changed for him. He makes it up as he goes along. I lock the door, go to the window, and open it a crack to let some air in. It's getting dark. The sun is going down on my first day of freedom in twenty years, and yet I'm terrified. I grab the pack of cigarettes the beautiful auburn-haired girl picked out for me and find my vodka. Larry has swilled down over half my booze. I light up a cigarette and lie down with the bottle. They're a good brand—"Thank you, my love." The vodka and the cigarettes are soothing. I kick off my shoes and eventually fall asleep.

* * *

What time is it? How long have I been asleep? I panic, reorient myself, and take a drink from the bottle on the bedside table. Is it past eleven? Where the hell am I? Veronica—maybe she's come and gone? The Beaumont—I know where I am. I remember seeing a clock at the front desk. Time has always been enforced, regulated. I need to buy a watch. Downstairs, no one is around. I check the clock. It's either nine or five minutes to ten. I can't tell. The clock is numberless. I go back to my room. If this girl, this cousin, is coming over, she'll be here soon. I close the window, straighten the sheets on the bed, turn on the television, and stare at the bad reception.

I'll shower and clean myself up—get ready—that's all I can think of to do. I turn the TV off, grab my toothbrush and toothpaste, and head out of my room.

The bathroom is at the end of the hall, close to the kitchen. Like the kitchen, it's worn out. There're four stalls that look to be in rough shape. I go in—urinate, flush—and see myself in the mirror and almost laugh. I can't believe any of it. I take my clothes off and go into a private shower (very rough shape). I run the water. I can't

believe any of it. Where I am, the clothes on the floor, my vodka and
cigarette breath, the Beaumont, the twenty years gone, the food in
the dresser drawers. I stand in the shower and don't move. It's my
first alone in decades, and I have no soap, no shampoo. There's no
towel waiting for me either. I don't have to watch my wrinkled ass. No
guard by the door. I keep opening up the shower curtain, looking out
to see if anyone is there—there isn't. And who is this woman coming
over? Veronica. Who is she? What does she know about me? I don't
know what she expects from me. I'll wait it out in the shower. Wait
her out. Hide out in here until she's come and gone. I'm an old man.
Larry's set me up—if in fact she is coming at all. If only Veronica were
the store clerk. She's kind. She gives me cigarettes. She's beautiful.
If only all women were like that. I want to call her Mira Rose. In
memory of my first love, the one that's gone.

Then the unthinkable happens. The kiss of death in jail. I
tremble, erect. My breathing comes out in short, quivering gasps.
What excites me? My freedom? The anticipation of night? I look
down at the strangeness of my old grey body and turn the hot water
off and the cold water on full. Now I am truly shivering and gasping.
Ice-cold. My flesh surrenders to it. I reach my breaking point. Turn
off the water. Search for my clothes on the floor and retrieve my pants
and shirt. Force them on. The material clings to me. I step out. Brush
my teeth and leave the bathroom. I leave footprints on the carpet as I
walk down the hall. I find my key, and go in.

I feel better being back in my room. I strip and throw my wet
clothes into the closet. My skin is wet and my hair drips water onto
my shoulders and down my back. I take a pillowcase off a pillow and
dry myself as best I can. I throw the pillowcase into the closet with
the clothes and close the door. I get dressed, sit on the bed, and light
a cigarette—smooth. I run my fingers through my hair. It's damp
and tangled, but I have no comb. I sweep my hair back and push my
fingers through the knots until my hand moves freely without getting
caught.

Maybe I should look for Larry—one floor up, room twelve.
I wish I had never run into the bastard. All I want is to finish my
cigarettes, down my vodka, and sleep. I butt out a cigarette, and leave
my room. Tonight isn't the night. I go to the end of the hall, find the
stairs, and go up. On the move again. Going in circles. Testing the
waters, waiting for them to lock me up and take away my key.

The fourth floor is exactly like the third and probably exactly

like the first, second, and fifth. I find room twelve. The door is slightly
open. I pause...push the door gently.

"Larry, you're gonna have to tell Veronica—"

"Tell her what?" a woman's voice cuts in.

"Jesus, I'm in the wrong room."

"You looking for Larry?" the woman calls.

I peek back in.

"You got the right room," she says. "He's down in the john."
She laughs, sits on the bed, counting a stack of bills—fives and tens.
A cigarette burns in an ashtray beside her. She sits with her legs
crossed, her skirt high up on her thighs. "Come on in," she continues.

"No, I'll...let you finish whatever..." I shut the door and hear
the woman calling after me as I go on down the hall.

"You don't have to go."

I keep up a good pace down the hall and pass the bathroom. It
stinks. I'm back on the stairs, back on my floor, back in my room, and
back in my bed. My heart pounds. Ten minutes pass. There's a knock
on the door. It opens.

"You Francis?" asks the woman. I sit up on the bed. "I'm
Veronica. What did you wanna tell me, honey?"

"I'm Francis," I tell her awkwardly.

"Nice to meet you." She walks into the room and closes the
door. I stand up.

"You're Larry's cousin?" I ask. She examines the card with the
deformed bird on my dresser.

"Yeah," she laughs, "if you can believe it. Anything to drink?"

She has a coarseness to her that I recognize. Yet she's completely
foreign to me. I like the sound of her voice and the look of her body.

"Some vodka." I go to the dresser. Veronica steps aside and
watches me open a drawer and find the bottle.

"What else you got in there?" She sits down on the bed.

"I got cake."

"Cake?"

I give her the vodka and go back in for the cake. I put the cake
beside her on the bed. She drinks from the bottle.

"How are we supposed to eat it? With our hands?"

I grab a fork and offer it to her.

"Mmm," she says and takes the fork and digs in.

I watch. She takes large hunks of cake and shoves them into
her mouth—chews, swallows. Then brings the bottle to her lips and

takes long swills. I watch. She sits on the bed and works without looking at me. She lets out a small moan. Then a tiny gasp. I light up a cigarette and try not to stare. Am I the envy of the boys back in lockup? Veronica stops and wipes her mouth, then takes another long, hard drink from the bottle.

"Ah! I needed that." She hands me the bottle. I take a drink. She picks up the cake, puts it on the floor, and sucks some icing off her fingers.

"Wow…" She throws her arms up over her head and falls backwards on the bed. The springs rattle. I see up her skirt. "That was the best goddamn cake from an old man's dresser I ever had," she laughs.

I take another look then another drink.

"So Larry says you sell insurance," she says. "Is that right?"

"Uh…yeah, right." I look away.

"What's that like?"

"Pretty good, I guess."

Larry has lied to her. Why has he said that? Why has he said anything?

"It's a strange business. It keeps me on the move."

I do my best with the lies.

"Yeah, I bet."

She holds her breath and then lets out a laugh.

"I'm just messing with you, man. I know you're a con."

Her joke is lost on me—uptight. I feel confused, stupid. Frustrated. Veronica continues to laugh and maintains a giggle between her words. My frustration grows with each laugh.

"He told me not to say anything," her words run together, "but I know you're a killer." She stops.

I take a hard drink of vodka and remain motionless.

"Isn't that right, baby? Eh? Tell momma how you kill."

Her tone is different now. Less mocking. This is a seduction. I watch as she begins taking off her clothes.

"You probably beat them to death with your bare hands, don't you?"

She is lost inside her own monologue and tosses from one side of the bed to the other, almost fully nude.

"Are you an animal, Francis?" she asks.

I watch her closely. She gets up off the bed and walks over to me. I drink from the empty bottle.

"Put that bottle down," she says. I do. "And show me what kind of an animal you are."

She switches off the light over by the door. Takes my hand and brings me to the bed. She lies down. I step into the mangled chocolate cake, slip, and fall on top of her. My elbow jabs into her stomach.

"Jesus." She breaks character.

"Fuck...geez." I pull away.

"Relax, relax." She brings me close.

I tremble on top of her naked body. My foot is covered in chocolate.

"Let yourself go." She tries to be tender. "Just like riding a bicycle."

She takes my hand and brings it to her chest.

"Relax. Let yourself go."

Her voice is seductive again. Any move I make elicits a response from her—a moan or a "there you go." I drag my hand along her body. I feel the numbness take over; it starts down in my legs then moves to my arms and shoulders through my back and down my ass. She reaches up and touches my face softly. I lose it, gyrate three times, bang my knee on the wall, gasp, shudder twice, twitch in spasm, then stop. It's over.

I lie on my side with my back to her. Still. She doesn't speak. Five minutes pass in silence. I don't know if I wish she would say something or am glad that she doesn't say a thing. She gets up. I can hear her stumbling around looking for her clothes. I don't move. Should I let her go? She goes to the door, pauses, unlocks, and opens it.

"Thanks for the cake, Francis." There isn't an ounce of sarcasm in her voice—she means to be kind. "Congratulations on getting out... good night."

She's gone.

I let out a sigh that's almost a whimper, "Goddamn you, Larry. Good night."

It's gonna take kindness for me to pull through. Yes, kindness and vodka. I fall asleep.

* * *

There's a knock at the door. I shoot straight up. I'm hungover, bleary-eyed, and still in my clothes. It's morning. I go to the door. There's dried chocolate cake between my toes. How long have I slept?

I open the door.

"Good morning," says a man.

Who the fuck is he? Where am I?

"You made it through your first night," he says.

He carries a large box marked *Logan*. He's in his mid-thirties and has dark black hair and a handsome face. He's powerfully built and moves well. It's Bates.

"Sleep well?" he asks. He puts the box on the dresser.

"Okay." I rub my face.

"Gonna offer me any of that cake?" He laughs.

I shove the cake under the bed with my foot and pull the sheets back. My mind goes to last night. The horror of last night, that tragic-comic freak show of last night.

"I brought some clothes," he says.

He opens the box, pulls out a red wool sweater. He's confident and sure in his actions. He carries his badge and gun well hidden. It's a wonder he's even a cop. He seems too human.

"I hope you can use them." He gestures to me. "This is probably the best thing in here."

He gives me the sweater. It looks new. I take the sweater and put it on immediately. A new uniform. It fits well but clashes with my brown, baggy hobo pants.

"There you go...that's pretty good." He's pleased. "There's a bunch of stuff. I'll leave the box, and you can take what you like."

"Okay." My head throbs.

He looks around the room and records the surroundings in his head with great detail. Over to the window, he pulls back the curtain. Light pours in and a ray of dust appears from the sun's beam.

"Like the place?" he asks.

I look up and our eyes lock for a moment. I look away. Bates' blue eyes aren't interested in the room at all. They carry the real questions and truly read the scene. Mine are bloodshot, scared.

"I don't blame you if you hate it," he says. "Just to get you on your feet."

I look down to the chocolate on my right foot. A crust has formed over the skin and it cracks with every movement. I go to the dresser and pull out a pair of blue socks. Where did the bologna come from? The day after getting out—what's the morning to a free man? And with Bates here, what's really changed? And with that botched romance, where's the possibility of the sweetness of a woman? No Mira Rose. Freedom's a fucking trap.

"Thought I might take you down to the zoo to have a look around before your first shift." He does a full turn inside the room. The smell of the place is in his clothes slightly, like his morning cologne is in the room a little. "Maybe some breakfast first," he adds.

I take his words like orders. He's stronger. He's still the jailer in spite of the kindness. Shoes, keys, the sweater warm enough to act as a coat.

We eat pancakes and eggs at the zoo's rest spot. See a gorgeous zoo waitress. Pick up a uniform from Harris in charge of grounds keeping, and record visit one—a success.

* * *

I've been here six weeks. Mud covers the grounds. Mud and wild manure. The snow is gone and the grass is growing. Patches of bright green peek through the earth like sporadic body hair. It's spring. I'm almost done my training. There's a great enthusiasm among my coworkers that I can't say I share. Everyone works tirelessly. I work hard but without the good cheer and thankfulness-to-be-alive smile of most. Maybe it's my age. I have at least two decades over all of them—three or more over many. There's Lynn and Trevor and Kate and Bill and Bill's brother Mike, and Doctors Roe through Blanchfield, also John with the bad leg who works the gift shop and Elise with the tight uniform who works admissions, and then there are the animals: Lucy and Lulu and Bebe and Walter and Peppo and so forth and so on. I've been introduced to new people and animals every day, most of whom I never see again or can't remember meeting. I'm always being introduced to new creatures. New faces. Eager faces. People who love the "zoo talk" and the smells and the rawness of the place. People who can't get enough of the place. Who love animals and talk to them and have nicknames for them like "Uncle Archie" or "Doo-little Dinkins." I hear that Bill calls one zebra "sweetheart." They have different names for every beast. But it's not the people I'm worried about. It's the animals in the cages. I can always feel them staring at me.

I'm known at the park as the old guy who seldom speaks. I keep to myself. I've become a part of the background. I change water buckets, transfer hay, deliver shipments of food, help prepare habitats, plant trees, shovel dung (loads of dung), and maintain walkways and glass barriers. The hardest thing is riding the carts, the zoo-mobiles. They're white golf carts painted up in various animal motifs. We use them to get around the park. I almost rolled the Hippo Cart once and since then, whenever I drive, it's always at a cautious, slow pace. I'm out of practice. This is another thing I'm known for: the old, shy guy who drives slow. But I don't give a shit. I like pacing myself. I've done a thousand different yet identical "work-details" in prison. I'm good at taking orders, repeating tasks, going with the flow.

I work days and some nights when they need me. I get a paycheque every other week. I take a bus to and from work. I get my routine down: daily chores in the morning, lunch break at noon, training in the afternoon. There's a schedule in the staff room that lists what new responsibilities I'm supposed to learn each day. Today, I'm going to be trained in the monkey den. This, hopefully, will complete my orientation and bump me up ten cents an hour in pay. I'm eating a roast beef and mustard sandwich. I finish the sandwich and head out to the south side of the park.

The monkeys have their own compound. I go inside. It's a mock habitat that regulates and simulates a tropical climate. Real exotic trees grow there. The air inside is thick and the stench is awful. Light comes through large glass windows in the ceiling—skylights from thirty feet above. There are long stretches of glass that separate the viewing area from where the monkeys live. Walkways run up and down in between the enclosures. It's noisy as hell. There's a large group of kids on a class trip, swarming the cages.

I avoid the kids and enter a door marked "Zoo Staff only." I find Jamie, one of my trainers. He's tall and slim and has a full beard. He's gentle in everything he does. He sits cross-legged on the floor and is tending to a monkey in a cage. His long, bony knees stretch up high above the ground. He's slouched down and has a few fingers in the cage. He's feeding the animal some kind of leaf.

"He's taking a time out," he says. "He gets so worked up when big groups come around." Jamie has incredible patience and understanding, and he never seems down or annoyed. "This is Brutus," he says. "He's a teenager. He's in one of his moods."

"Sure," I say and go over to the couch and sit.

Brutus sees me and pulls away from Jamie. He stares at me and starts banging on the cage. The noise startles me, and I jump to my feet.

"Brutus," Jamie says calmly.

Brutus lets out a piercing, high-pitched screech.

"He's just showing off," Jamie says. "He's a real ham. Brutus, this is Francis."

Brutus bangs the cage again and belts out another call.

"You better come and introduce yourself," he says. "He can go on for hours."

I approach cautiously.

"Brutus, be nice," says Jamie.

The monkey becomes still. We lock eyes. I look away. Brutus bangs the cage, and I move back to the couch. A woman comes in.

"Nancy, can you take over here?" asks Jamie. "Brutus needs some one-on-one, and I have to show Francis around."

Nancy looks exactly like Jamie but doesn't have a beard.

"Sure can," she says. She carries a bucket of banana peels. "How's my little rascal," she begins, and drops to the floor.

"Sorry, Francis." Jamie stands up. "Boys will be boys." I can hear his bones crack as he straightens up. "I'll show you around."

He leads me to the door. Before I leave, I glance over at Brutus in the cage. He's lying on his back with an arm out, and it seems like he's groping Nancy's breasts. He stares at me coolly as he plays. I leave the room.

There are five main sections to the den. The largest houses the common chimps, like that sexy bastard Brutus. One is reserved for mothers and babies. Two smaller dens are for gorillas and assorted other loaner monkeys visiting the zoo. The children on their trip form an awkward line. A frantic, red-faced teacher is at the head. Willis, their tour guide, shouts information about the monkeys over the voices of the children. It's a familiar scene to me.

Jamie begins his instruction:

"The most important thing about this particular habitat is to maintain the temperature and the air quality," he says. "This is the thermostat. It must stay at ninety degrees and never dip down past eighty. If it were to get out of control for long enough, the monkeys could get really sick—probably die."

He shows me how to read the apparatus and how to readjust the controls. I pay as much attention as I can. He leads me to a storage area. Inside are boxes of dried fruits and berries, stacks of hay, piles of leaves, and bushels of bananas spread out throughout the room.

"This, of course, is where we keep the food," he says. "Monkeys can be very fussy eaters."

He shows me the place: stockrooms, loading doors, medical facilities. It's fully functioning.

"Your duties will vary from day to day in here," he says.

"Cleanup can be heavy sometimes." I can tell he loves his job, and he's good at it. I follow him into an empty, glass-enclosed dwelling.

"There's no one living in here yet," he says. "We're anticipating territorial issues in the main den. This space will house those that need to be separated from the rest of the group." It's a playground for monkeys: trees, hay, ropes, swings with tires on the ends, and large rubber toys scattered about.

"As you can see," he says, "the place is a mess. The ground needs to be swept and sprayed, and all the hay has to be changed." He shows me where to find a broom and a bin and instructs me on how to use the water hose.

"Any questions?"

"No, I think I got it," I tell him.

He smiles.

"Good, if you need anything, please, we're a team here."

He's sincere. He leaves me to my work—basically monkey shit. I begin by sweeping up all the soiled hay and dumping everything into the large bin. I pile up the rubber toys. Find banana peels mashed into some of them. I untangle ropes and remove hay and dirt from the swing tires. I'm in a trance. Am I really here? I look up and see a group of grade six boys gathered on the other side of the glass, looking in.

"What kind of ape is this?" says one of them. They laugh. "Hey, where's your fur, man?"

It takes me a minute to realize that they're staring at me. I go on working.

"Come on, do a trick for us, man."

More children join. They press their faces against the glass. Some kick it with their boots. I keep my head down and start screwing in the water hose. There're about twenty kids looking in now. I stay on task.

"Nice hose, old man!"

Where's the fucking teacher? I turn the water on and begin spraying down the den. The children keep staring at me and bang harder on the glass. I lose control of the hose for a minute and spray myself in the face, then in the crotch of my pants. The children go wild. I regain control.

"He pissed himself," a boy yells at the top of his lungs. The children repeat the phrase. "He pissed himself. The bald ape pissed himself."

The laughter won't stop. I turn the hose towards the glass. The children scream with delight and make to shelter themselves from the water. I'm surprised at the result. A teacher comes over and gives me a dirty look from the other side. She starts collecting the children and attempts to calm them down. I turn off the water and push the bin of hay out of the den. I pass the children. They've moved on to another spectacle in another den. An enormous ape (a real one) is eating a banana. The children watch and yell things at him. He shows no sign of caring. He's a massive creature with a powerful body. He must weigh over four hundred pounds. I walk by. The ape rises suddenly and goes against the glass. I stop and look at him. He squints and stares right at me. A sign over the window reads 'Grover.' He starts pacing on his knuckles from one side of the den to the other, chewing his food. Grover stops eating the banana and shoots another intense glare at me. He pauses, then spits the banana into each one of his hands and smears it on the glass. The children scream out in astonishment and glee. I walk away.

As I leave the monkey house, I see Brutus again—now inside the main den with the others. He's masturbating wildly.

* * *

I get off the bus and walk into my building, my zoo clothes and zoo boots still on. I'm covered with nature. I give a superficial stomp on the welcome mat and go upstairs to my room. A couple has moved in next door. They fight constantly; and, if they're not fighting, they're make some kind of banging noise. Walking by, I can't tell if the sounds are of love or hate. I go into my room. I turn on the shortwave radio my parole officer has given me and drown them out. I keep the radio on as much as I can. It seems to help. The TV never works. I like listening to foreign stations that play exotic music, and I appreciate not understanding the announcers when they speak. A bossa nova plays. I remove my dirty uniform and throw it in a pile on the floor. I lie down and light up a cigarette.

The episode with the monkeys has made me realize how unpredictable things can get at that place. I always feel the threat. The snakes and the wild cats, and the polar bears and the apes. Somehow the presence of people walking around from exhibit to exhibit with their kids or friends or teachers or spouses distracts the others, but I feel their eyes. Maybe I'm the only one they look at.

I get up and pour myself a drink. A samba plays. I get dressed. Larry is coming over for a poker game, and he's bringing a friend from the fifth floor—Johnston. The two have done time together years ago. I finish my drink. I'm going to have to buy beer and snacks for the game. Larry always cleans me out whenever he comes over. I don't care. What the hell else are my paycheques good for? Besides, it gives me an excuse to go visit Mira Rosa.

My Mira Rose is the beautiful girl who works at The Food Depot across the street. She's the subtle beauty who was put on earth to comfort the wretched of the world. She's deserving of all my love. Her family owns the store, owns her. She works part-time. I go there constantly. I haven't yet figured out a way to see her away from the place. She always makes me feel welcome and talks with me or throws smiles at me from across the store if she's busy. Sometimes when the place is empty, she walks with me and helps me pick out my groceries. I follow her up and down the aisles and nod at all of her suggestions.

She's in her last year of high school—young, kind, ageless. She makes things bearable. In fact, she's the only thing that does. A touch of wonder to keep off the madness.

I hate lying to her about my past. I mumble something about being a retired carpenter when she asks. Maybe I could have been. But I tell her all about my new job at the zoo. She in turn tells me about the problems she's having with her family and stuff at school and her fears about the future and once about her dreams. I listen to her like she's the only sound on earth. Is it fair that such things so beautiful can blind me from the misery of it all?

I walk in and look around; the place is full. I see Mira Rose at the checkout and wait until she notices me. She smiles and waves. I nod and go seek out some pork rinds for Larry. I grab a bag of rinds, a bag of salt peanuts, and some pretzels, and take my place at the back of her checkout line. Mira Rose works with a contented look on her face—grace-filled. But a look that knows or at least understands sadness—it must—to be so perfect and calm and wise. She has vanilla skin and big, brown eyes. She's that kind of girl I always think about, and always will.

A huge man wearing an apron comes out from the back and opens up another register.

"Can I help who's next please," he says.

His apron is stained with blood—probably the butcher. A lady in front of me goes to the new checkout. I remain in Mira Rose's line. She's working on a large purchase. The bloody man finishes with the woman and calls to me.

"Can I help who's next, please."

I don't move.

"Sir," he goes on, "can I help you here."

My heart groans.

"I want to…"

"She's busy," he says firmly.

I look at him. His eyes are cold. I change lanes. Who is he? A beast with two large arms, a massive head, a massive chest, and a gorilla belly. He checks out the snacks.

"You live across the street, don't you?" he says.

I look up.

"That's right."

I feel the threat.

"That'll be $7.50."

I pay him and go to the exit. I pass Mira Rose but don't try for her attention. I hear the man call out, "can I help who's next please," and go buy some beer.

* * *

None of us take the game seriously. We use cigarettes to bet with. It's safer this way. Even drunk, we won't argue over lost cigarettes. Besides, it's the way it's done in prison. The cards belong to Larry. They're old with pictures of naked girls on the back. The game is Seven Card Stud.

"Do you remember that son-of-a-bitch guard who got fired for sleeping with the warden's daughter?" Larry laughs.

He's a social animal. He thrives in the company of others. I've already heard the story twice, but don't mind hearing it again. We play on.

"His name was Vetz or Getz, what was it? Francis, do you remember?" he asks.

I don't, on purpose. I don't want to tell him.

"No, I don't," I say.

"Vetzel! Mike Vetzel I think. Anyway," Larry says, downing some peanuts, "this guy Vetzel was a real piece a work. A real ladies' man. A Casanova. And rumour had it that he was quite well built, you know, huge. Women all over him. He was good looking too. Most of the guards were uglier than sin, but this Vetzel had a nice face, you know, clean. Looked more like a movie star than a guy caging cons."

Larry stops to gulp some beer.

"And so the other guards would always tease him about his

appearance and good looks, but nobody teased him more than...
the warden," Larry bellows. He's already delivered the punch line.
"They called him a pretty boy and that, but he was a good sport and
always took it like a man. And when they'd ask him about his latest
lay, he'd always go into intense detail. Try to gross them out. He'd
tell everybody what kind of weird kinky shit he was into with girls.
Chains and dog food and...sick stuff, really sick stuff. But the guards
loved it. They ate it up. And nobody more than..."

He awaits a response.

"The warden!" Johnston catches on.

"The warden, right. So this went on and they keep asking about
the woman, and Vetzel keeps telling these freak show stories. Until
one day, Vetzel calls in sick. Says he'd better stay home and rest."

Larry rolls his eyes.

"What's wrong with him?" Johnston asks.

"Nothing." Larry is losing his crowd. "He isn't sick. He doesn't
stay home. This starts happening every week; every Friday, he calls in
sick. And people start getting suspicious, but they all like the guy too
much to say anything. Until one Friday, the warden decides to kick
off early. And when he gets home and goes upstairs who does he find
in his house dressed up in this leopard leotard with holes cut out of
the front? Vetzel! In his eighteen-year-old's bedroom!"

Larry howls. Johnston gasps then roars. I laugh too.

"What was she wearing?" Johnston asks.

"I don't know, a smile."

We're off again, laughing and coughing in between. It's a good
time and we all break even and all get drunk and play until all the
cigarettes are ashes. Larry tells other stories, but I don't recognize
any of them. Names of guards and inmates, meals, fights that break
out in the prison, the smell of the place, and people he's seen die in
there. It's all so hazy; I can't distinguish one detail from another. My
memories sit inside of me somewhere at the centre. They are present
in everything I do. I know it, but I'm unable to bring them to the
surface.

"Hey, why don't you tell us about some of your sex crimes,
Francis?" Larry says, drunk. "The one that landed you in the
slammer."

I don't respond. I keep my head down. The fat pig's wasted
again. He forgets his suggestion and moves to another topic about a
score he's close to.

"Real straight forward. We basically walk in and take the stuff," he says.

Johnston bobs his head in agreement. Larry goes on about some shipment coming to some warehouse. And he knows a guy on the inside, a brother-in-law or someone related. And they are gonna get their hands all over some fine, easy-to-move merchandise. I don't pay any attention to him. He's a small-time thief, always pushing a new scheme, constantly gossiping about deals he's making and jobs he's heard about. He's a low-key player on the underground who never loses hope, dreaming about the one really big score he'll land one day.

"Think about it," he says and gets up from where he's sitting. Crumbs fall off him. "Wow, I better head on up."

He moves solidly to the door. Johnston follows.

"Yeah, I'd better head up too," Johnston says.

I'm glad Larry has himself a sidekick. It means I won't have to feel bad about always saying no to his propositions. The two men burp and scratch their way out of the room.

"See ya later."

"See ya later."

They're gone. I turn on a cool Latin waltz and pass out faced down on my bed. In other beds somewhere, all those nameless friends back in jail are lying awake writing letters by candlelight in their cells. And Brutus is lying with Grover and the others in the hay. And Mira Rose is dreaming of open fields at night. And the memories of nights passed in horror are silent and still inside of me—"God help us."

* * *

Everybody loves the dolphins. I'm at the performance tank where two bottlenose twins perform a routine in water for a small capacity crowd. It's a tiny arena that holds about seventy-five people—a kind of aquatic theatre. The two mammals, Janet and Ben, have trainers—people—Mindy and Lou, dressed in tight-fitting wet suits, who hold up dead fish for the dolphins. They jump up, grab the food, and swim around for the crowd who cheer and yell for more. I resist watching the whole show as long as I can.

I'm hanging out at the gate. People are out in droves. There's no semblance of order or a decent lineup. They're pushing through to find their seats. It makes me sick. I'm trying to remain unnoticed, but I can't quite handle the rush of the crowd. I'm standing back and out of the way. The show is a spectacle. I'm fed up with this goddamn place.

With the elephants that charge me, the lions that roar, the snakes that hiss, the hyenas that laugh at me, the wild horses bucking, and the monkeys never backing off, I'm tested more and more every day. Everyday, I see a new pair of eyes on me—a new threat. I don't trust the cages. I'm constantly looking behind me as I walk through the zoo. I peek around bushes and test the fences and locks. I carry a small pocket knife with me for protection, hidden in my right boot. I'm getting used to the smell.

The show starts. A door opens up in the tank and the dolphins swim in. The audience is enthused, and rises to get a better look. A few children run towards the pool. Next, the trainers run in. The audience applauds and an announcer on a megaphone begins. Statistics about Ben and Janet are given in detail: they're two years old, brother and sister, acrobats by nature, performers by trade. They have the same brain-to-body ratio as humans, and they are gregarious in all that they do. I keep my head down.

The person in row eight, seat 4B is chosen to get a kiss from one of the dolphins. The lucky young girl is hoisted up and Ben swims to her and launches himself into the air, tongue first. The audience is charmed and applauds loudly. I can't help feeling the terror of the scene. The girl runs back to her seat, and the show plays on.

Between the tuna-tango and the endless round of figure eights, I wander off. I take breaks from time to time. After I finish at an exhibit—scooping something or filling something—I disappear for a while. Go unnoticed. A supervisor catches me once, and I tell him I'm lost. There're so many people working at the place and so much space and so much to do. I find it easy to slip away.

I stop in at the petting zoo area. It's usually a good place to hide out. There are four separate barns and a few sheds that look out onto patches of viewing fields enclosed by wooden fences. A mini-course gives pony rides. And for twenty-five cents a handful, you can buy corn to feed the animals. I pull up behind a small shed. Inside are rabbits, chickens, and other birds. It's a poorly attended spot. Even the goats and donkeys get more of an audience.

I sit down on the grass. I feel old. My body has never been worked as hard. I have aches and pains all over. My hands, which have always been soft, are calloused now, and I must have arthritis in more than three different joints. I recognize nothing. I know nothing. I wish I could enjoy the openness of the place—so calm and peaceful—but my nerves are all but shot. I pull out a pack of cigarettes and light up.

A pig comes around to the edge of the fence and watches me smoke. He is an enormous pink mother of a pig with a thick coat of fur. I find him strange. The pig's covered in shit, appropriately, and sniffs the air with his snout. What does he want? I keep my eyes glued to him, but he gives no signs of a threat. Instead, he moves closer, and it looks as though he's enjoying the scent from the Marlboro regulars. I inhale and blow smoke into the pig's face; he closes his eyes and sucks back the air. He lies down on his back and extends his potbelly. Old udders protrude. I pin him at 150, 200 pounds, at least. The two of us look up and take in the blueness of the sky. We stay this way for ten minutes.

I hear the sound of a gate opening. I jump up. The pig rises to attention. We look at one another and go our separate ways, the pig back to his pen and me around to the other side of the shed. I see a worker with a feed bucket (either Ross or Andy). I toss my cigarette butt away and walk over to the main walkway, unnoticed. Apart from his pleasant ways, the pig reminds me of a constable I think I knew once. Before he's completely out of sight, I look back and see constable-pig in the distance slurping down some feed. I head back to the fish.

* * *

They are on their grand finale, which looks remarkably similar to their opening swim-and-flip routine. I find the show entirely draining. They end in a flurry of gyrations and synchronized calls. They splash hard in the water and everyone in the first two rows gets wet. They scream with delight. I'm one of these lucky ones; my coveralls cling to me, drenched.

"Alright, Ben and Janet!"

The audience claps. The dolphins bow.

"How about their trainers!"

The audience goes on. Mindy and Lou bow.

It's done. The stage is cleared and the water settles. The people continue to praise the performance to one another as they spill out of the arena. I'm lost in the crowd and feel the crush. The people keep coming. They all have similar comments, and everyone wishes they got a kiss, and they retell stories of dolphins helping lost fishermen at sea. I try to remain still as they push past me on to another exhibit. Mindy comes out, still in her tight wetsuit. She is a magnificent creature.

"Hey, Francis, how was the show?" she asks.

I look up. She looks like a deep-sea diver after a successful treasure hunt.

"Great, real good," I nod.

"Aren't they dolls?"

"Yeah." I must seem awestruck.

"I'll never get over how smart they are," she says and moves to meet some fans.

It's a dizzying experience. I feel short of breath. I leave the arena. Where are the dolphins now? Back in their dressing rooms, discussing the merits of their individual performances? I head over to check on the water situation at the giraffe habitat.

A Tiger Cart comes barrelling towards me.

"Get in," the driver says. It's Rod, a colleague. "I'll brief you on the way."

His face is red, and he's pumped up on some news.

"What's happening?" I ask. I don't appreciate his driving.

"Fire," he says. "In the petting zoo. Don't know how big. Don't know who's down." Rod speaks in an abridged cop lingo. "We need all the men we can get."

I hold on for the ride. The pit that is my stomach widens and echoes. I see a crowd gathered by the chicken shed. Workers are moving bunnies and birds out in individual cages, while others move in a bucket brigade. Somewhere, someone has a hose. There are no flames, just a few plumes of smoke coming out of the shed. I look on in horror. The panic rouses the other animals, who send out calls of anguish and fear. I keep my distance but try to get a handle on the situation. I cross the fence into the yard. Cages of animals are collected outside the shed, and I examine them. Some turkeys; fine. A few chickens; fine. A rooster, rabbits. Everything seems unharmed. I ease up a little. The damage is minimal—some darkened feathers and fur. The buckets stop. The hose is turned off. There is no smoke now. A siren signals the arrival of the fire department, but it's all over. A crowd of people catches wind of the incident and begins to set up watch around the fence. Workers hold them off.

A tall woman comes out of the shed with black ash on her forehead and underneath her eyes. She carries what looks like a tiny chick in both hands. The creature is in a ball, motionless, grey, and quite obviously dead. The fire department moves in and asks everyone to clear out. I watch the dead chick being carried off until it's out of sight. I'm stunned. I remain motionless by the fence. My mouth is open and my eyes are sunk back into my head. I look down at the mud

on my boots. The pig trots over to me. Glares at me. Walks off. Then
Rod touches my shoulder.

"Man, what the hell was that?" Rod's angry.

We move away from the area.

"Can you believe that?" he asks.

"Is that bird dead?"

"They think a cigarette started the damn thing."

His outrage is clear. He hasn't seen much horror in life.

"I mean, think about what could have happened if that thing
spread. The whole damn place could have gone up. Some barbecue
that would be."

He doesn't mean to be funny.

"What about the bird?" I ask.

"What about it? It's dead...Francis, it's dead! Want a lift?" he
asks.

"No, you go ahead," I say.

Rod continues to make comments under his breath and drives
away in the Tiger Cart. I stay to watch the fire department secure
the location and talk to some zoo officials. I'm numb. I can't escape
it. A peacock approaches the edge of the fence, and I move in to get
a better look. It's gorgeous. It spreads an enormous fan of blues and
purples and orange. My eyes light up. I reach over the fence and grab
hold of one of its feathers, pull hard and pluck one out. The peacock
reels back and closes its fan. I'll give the feather to Mira Rose.

On my way out, I hear reports of the fire from different workers.
Some are more realistic in their descriptions than others. The chick
is dead. Some say his name is Arthur, some say Angus. A cigarette
did indeed start the fire. An investigation is underway, but it looks as
though two teenage boys are to blame. They were found goofing off
by the fountains and caught with a pack of cigarettes. It seems that
no one has bothered to question the pig.

What the hell can I feel? I'm riding home in a daze. The image
of that dead bird is alive in my head, and the thought of that fat
eyewitness rolling around in the shit and piss haunts me. I let the boys
take the fall on this one. This is an arson rap I can't afford. Murder
two for sure—slaughter without intent. I'll never confess.

* * *

More sirens. This time in front of the Beaumont. I get off the bus and
approach the situation with caution. I've seen enough carnage for one
day. Enough for fifty lifetimes. And I know I'll see more. And yes, I

know the victim. I always do. Larry's strapped onto a stretcher. Three medics half his size work on getting him into an ambulance. Manny stands out front with his arms folded. There are people gazing at the scene from their windows. I see most of my neighbours for the first time: rejected faces, with mad eyes and bodies that are either hollow or spilling over—stuffed. Turpentine mouths and worn bone temples.

I feel the eyes of the neighbourhood.

"Do you know this man, sir?" a medic asks me.

"Yes."

I smell the vomit on Larry's shirt. They get him into the cab.

"Are you gonna ride with him?"

His voice is hurried but calm. I don't respond. I take his question like an order and get inside. I'm sitting on a tiny stool. Larry has an oxygen mask on. The straps of the stretcher are pulled tight against his body. The ambulance drives away. Its siren pierces down the street. I'm calm. I stare at the inside of the vehicle. There's a built-in shelving unit that holds supplies: blankets, boxes, jars of clear liquid, a heart monitoring machine, traffic pylons, and emergency equipment. Are these the things needed to save a life? I look down at the patient. Our eyes meet briefly. We acknowledge the inevitable. Every dog has his day, man.

We are at the hospital. I wait with Larry. The emergency room is a freak show of disease and heartache, with all the stress and all the calls for painkillers falling on deaf ears. I'm deep inside to block them out. Larry's out cold. He looks much more peaceful. I hear someone say he's a victim of cardiac arrest or something similar-sounding. Everything goes on in a kind of frenzied order. The hospital staff are in professional mode—calm. I'm calm—focused. Like Larry and all the other cases in the room that don't stand a chance. The panic comes from the people who are nowhere near death. Or the people who can't stand losing someone. The weak. The ones who are about to go seem quite content to me. They have a lot less to worry about. But the ones with busted arms or slashed wrists or the people walking away from the head-on collisions or gang wars, they are the ones who won't shut their mouths. Protesting life, not death. The ones who accept their suffering will be relieved soon enough.

They take Larry away. I find a seat next to some poor heroin addict. We don't speak. A nurse gives me a pen and a clipboard with forms attached. First name: Larry. Last name: I can't remember. Address: 181 Beaumont. Telephone: unknown. Occupation: Pimp or janitor or ex-con or comedian. Weight: Fat. Height: Medium. Age: 150. Species: Homo sapiens. Hobbies: Sadness, beer, poker. What the fuck can I say?

I stop reading the forms. What do I know about him? What does this information matter? I'm staring at a cancer prevention poster on the wall; it's a diagram of a cyst and has notes about dangerous-looking moles and lumps. What haven't I already seen? Time is cancer.

A doctor comes out and notes the zoo on my boots. Then tells me Larry's dead.

"Have you finished the forms?" he asks.

I say he'll have to get somebody else to fill out the last section concerning Larry's life insurance plan. I hand the clipboard to the doctor, leave the emergency waiting room, and get out of that hospital as fast as I can, out into the street to look for the nearest bus stop.

* * *

The excitement in front of my place is over now. There's no one around. I carry the peacock's purple feather in my right hand. I cross the street for some beer. In memory of Larry's liver. I pass the grocery store and look in. The divine Mira Rose is still working. The human gorilla is working too. Maybe I should go in, give her the feather, and leave. Maybe I should free that beautiful creature from the arms of that gorilla-ass motherfucker—the butcher. But something tells me to avoid danger.

Mira Rose's eyes light up when she sees me, I swear. I don't delay. I cross to her cash.

"What happened across the street?" Her tone is real concern.

"I brought you this," I say, and lay the feather down on the counter.

"Oh, it's beautiful," she says and picks up the bird's feather.

"My dearest, my love," I whisper.

"It's beautiful, Francis," she says. "Thank you."

I turn around. I'm gone. I carry out my mission successfully. I'm next door. I buy the beer and bring it home. I strip. Turn on the radio. Lie down. Drink the beer. Stare at the walls. Sleep.

* * *

We're sitting at a booth with our usual meals: buttermilk pancakes, bacon and eggs on the side, and a small dish of fresh fruit. We sip coffee and avoid the small talk. It's a clear morning, and the sky's a perfect blue. We could be any two men sitting here at breakfast, not necessarily an ex-con and his parole officer. Any father and son, any

two friends, any master and slave. But what we are is an ex-con and
his parole officer.

"This new man taking over for me, Griffith, he's a fair man,"
Bates says. "I already put a good word in for you."

His voice is almost apologetic. I pour rich maple syrup on my
flapjacks and drown them. I love sweet things.

"I gotta be honest though," he says, chomping on some bacon,
"you're gonna have to start filling out those progress reports."

He never makes me fill them out; he never forces me to join any
social clubs, or goes after me for waking up drunk. I look up from my
plate. Go back to my food.

"They are a real pain I know. Just write how the day you just
finished was better than the day before it, and what you're going
to try to make the day to come better than the one you're in." He
pauses, and we look at each other. He laughs. "Say you'll try your
best, Francis." He's lighter now than before. "C'mon, tell me you'll be
all right, huh?"

He starts in on his eggs.

"Don't worry," I say. "I'll be fine."

"Good. Just six more months anyway...then you can do what
you like...within reason." He laughs again. "You might want to travel
around a bit; see the world."

The suggestion is unreasonable. "Move out of that halfway
house if it's getting to you. Don't lose hope."

I smile for him. He always treats me with respect. Tries to help.
Gives me the radio, a mini fridge, a new lamp, a sweater. Once he
introduced me to his family—his wife Jenny and their two boys Sal
and Dean. He's a good man, and I like him as much as I can a man.
It's sad to see him go. We eat.

"So how's the zoo?"

"Busy. Summer vacation."

"I bet. I'd take the boys, but I don't know if I could take the
smell."

"Tell me about it."

Bates laughs.

"Oh geez, sorry, Francis. I don't know how you do it."

What will happen if I tell Bates all about the zoo? About the
pig waiting to squeal on me and the fire and the dead bird. And the
crush of the people and how unsafe it is for me there. And all the
threats I've received from those bastards, those beasts in the cages.

"It has its moments," I say.

Bates feels the hesitation.

"Is there something wrong?" he asks.

"I've had a few close calls with some of the animals."

I wonder if he can help? I want to tell him. I need to.

"Like what?" He's back on his guard and ready.

I can't do it.

"Nothing, they're animals, they stink."

"Oh yeah, I can imagine."

He doesn't know shit, not without having been around it for so long.

"Sure." I throw it away. I can't even tell Bates. Who is kind to me. Who treats me well. Better than most.

"So you're leaving Saturday?" I ask.

"Saturday afternoon, that's right. God, we still have so much to pack." The domestic man comes out fully now. "Jenny is driving me nuts with this one. She wants to make sure everything is perfect and everything is labelled properly down to the exact room location and where in the room the stuff is supposed to end up. And the new house is twice as big as our old one, so I just know we'll be going out and buying new stuff anyway."

I smile again.

"I don't know how I'm gonna do it." Bates holds back his excitement but not his fears. "I don't know about B.C.," he says. "I mean Jenny grew up there. She has tons of family and friends there, but I...I don't know."

I wish I had some advice for him. How does he expect me to know that shit?

"Best of luck," I say.

"Yup, we'll see." Bates' mind is on the move. Packing up all his stuff and shipping it off; packing up his boys and his wife and flying away. Going across the country in search of happiness, if only his wife's.

A waitress comes by and Bates pays for the food. He reaches into his pocket.

"So I got this for you," he says plainly, and throws a tiny box on the table. "It's a lighter. I know you hate surprises."

My face goes red. I open the box. A silver Zippo without a contrived inscription, just my name on it: FRANCIS.

"Thanks, Charlie," I say.

"Yeah." He smiles.

"So look out for this Griffith, eh?" He pushes through the awkwardness and stands up. "I'm glad I met you, Francis." We shake hands. "Good luck."

"Same to you," I say.

"Absolutely. So, I'll see ya."

He does what he can. He turns around and is gone. I stay in my seat and look down at the gift.

I'll sleep the rest of the day. Call in sick. Lay low. Wait for the scene to cool down. Take it a day at a time. Start filling out those progress reports. Tell Mira Rose about my crime. Pay a visit to constable-pig tomorrow.

* * *

They put me on the night shift. I only work nights now. Maybe it's my appearance. My bloodshot eyes. My beard. My fingernails. I'm unfit to be seen by the patrons. At least they haven't taken me into a shed and sprayed me down with cologne. I like my coworkers better at night though. The ones allergic to daytime.

We move through the grounds with our flashlights, as the animals dream up nightmarish visions. I'm at the lions' den, filling up the water. I can hear them snoring. Rumbling from deep inside. The kings of the place. In every institution, one reigns supreme; here, it's the cats. I turn the water off. I'm winding up the hose. I hear him calling out in a whisper from deep inside his throat.

"Francis."

I keep my head down and stay on task.

"Francis. You fucking coward."

I hate cats. I spit in their water. My footsteps cut through a growl as I walk away.

There's a new zebra that just came in. I'm at his cage. He's down and asleep. Newsprint horse. I'm throwing down gravel around the cage. Tiny grey stones. A handful at a time. I let some go, and they fall inside the cage. He stirs.

"I heard about you," he says.

I look at him. I look away. I'm throwing stones more carefully now.

"Word is you're a punk. Worse than a baby killer."

I go inside the storage bunker beside the cage. I hear him calling.

"I'm talking to you, bitch. Punk-ass. I'll be watching."

I set down the sack of gravel and move out. The moon is out.

It's cold. The zoo's a few miles away from the city, near an open highway and nothing but fields. The wind busts through; currents pick up speed out here. They keep us away from the city in our own climate—our own city.

It's time for a late lunch. Honey on a loaf. I keep vodka in my coffee thermos. I bring a raw onion for that pig. I've been doing it for weeks to keep him happy. I'm at the barn. I knock three times. He moves out half-asleep. Walking like a playboy. I toss him the onion.

"How are you, Francis?" he says. "Give any good hand-jobs lately?"

He snorts back inside the barn. I hate being a slave to him. I'd like to slit his fat throat. I walk over to the south side of the park— the monkey den. I learn to defend myself—fight back. Inside, I turn the temperature down a few more notches, just enough to make the assholes uncomfortable. I move without sound. If I wake the bitches up, they'll start in on me. I set down my flashlight and my lunch bag. I go to Brutus's cage. I owe him one for the shit balls he's always flinging at me all week. I unzip my coveralls, whip it out, and piss in his hay. The gold stream covers his bed. A steam rises up. I hear a noise and zip up. I turn around. Grover has my lunch bag and is smiling at me from inside of his cage.

"No wonder, you can't keep a woman," he says. "You got the tiniest pecker I've ever seen."

He opens up my lunch with his idiot gorilla hands.

"Want it back, bitch?" he asks. "Open up the cage and get it."

He holds my food out through the bars. I don't have the key— motherfucker.

"Too bad." He moves back into a shadow in his cage. "Get your tiny prick out of my den, fucko, before I bite the thing off."

I move out of the monkey house. I'll shit in his straw tomorrow.

* * *

In zoo dreams, I talk to myself. In this one, I'm talking to Mira Rose's father, the butcher. Blood everywhere. Slaughtering pigs. Picture him coming at me with a meat cleaver. His body drenched in blood. He's her father. He's got the right. He has a daughter he'll probably butcher himself, like a lamb.

I don't like him. Spoiling my plan. He has other plans, this father. He's steeped in blood. Like Mr. Crummer, the father of my first love. Plans they conceive when their daughters are still unborn. If they let them live.

Forced to meet at night. Go to the woods. By the creek. Near the tracks. Or some lousy room. Talk. Cry. Hold each other. Ready to let go. The collapse begins. You don't eat. You don't sleep. Right. You see yourself as if on a TV screen. You want to love so much you could die. You want to die for love. For love. Then the idea—an image—comes into your head. And on the screen. There's no other way. The suicide pact. Together. Get away from the butchering fathers. Meet at the place. The ground that defends you. Walls. Mounds of dirt. And stars that break your heart and mountains that come crashing down on you the emptier you are. Killing her. But you can't finish it. You should've died first. She says she couldn't do it if it's that way. Her lifeless body in your arms. Your eventual arrest. Twenty years, a life...

"What are you doing here?" asks the butcher.

I don't respond. He's covered in blood. I'm in the alley at the back of the grocery store. He's probably looking for cats to kill. The way he looks at me, I know he's protecting Mira Rose. Paternal, hard.

"You shouldn't be back here," he says.

The smell of the dumpster is awful. The back steps are wet, sticky.

"Go around to the front," he says, "if you want groceries."

His threat is veiled. The veil slips away. Our eyes lock. I look away. Move away slowly. I step in blood. He slams the metal door and goes in.

The alley is narrow, dark. I can't walk away from what I want to do to him. For Mira Rose. We could meet somewhere. Away from here. But she's not coming out. Help me, Mira Rose. We have a lot to talk about, my love. A lot to do.

"Crumpecker," a cat meows.

I try not to listen to what he's calling me.

"Crumpecker."

I don't want to hear it anymore. My name is smeared in cat shit on the wall.

* * *

I don't visit Mira Rose anymore. Her father is a butcher in more ways than one. He doesn't want me around. He keeps her locked up, and she hates him for it. If only I could free her, take her away from it all. The beautiful don't belong beside the wretched. Unless, like me, the wretched worship the beautiful.

I'm at the liquor store. I drink to keep my mind sober. They know me in here. Eddie, the twenty-two-year-old kid behind the counter, knows me. He sees me every day. Sometimes two, three times a day. My ritual. He likes it when I compliment him on his cowboy boots. I can drink more and more every day. My blood accepts the stuff. It goes down smooth. I'm counting the change inside my pocket to see if I have enough for the full-size bottle of Crown Royal. She walks in. Mira Rose. She comes in from next door. I duck down behind a display of red wine bottles. She goes to the counter and embraces Eddie. He puts his arms around her tiny waist and his mouth to hers. Oh Eddie, you must not only be a boyfriend: you must be a slave. You're dead, Eddie, I say to myself. They laugh together and stare blindly into one another's eyes. Young love. But I know it to be lust, self-obsession with a touch of kindness.

She leaves the store. I buy a bottle of rum. Eddie's hard-on peeks through his pants. I'm in the street. This corner of mine is a comfortable hole. The butcher walks out of his store. He carries a huge load over his shoulder and brings it to the back of his van. He's probably butchering the neighbourhood animals and serving the meat. One of these days he's going to be found in the alley with his throat cut—his guts cut out.

Mira Rose is locking up the store. She turns the key with her tiny hands. Unplugs a chord and the light goes out. I see her move to her father. She touches his back with her hand. The beast thrusts his load into the van. He closes the back door. I see them in the alleyway together. Father and daughter. Jailer and prisoner. Mira Rose, my love, tell me what I can do (could have done) to set you free. I am here in front of the halfway house. But I am always convicted, always crucified, tortured in your heart. To live, I must love the world. To love the world is to love you. To love you is to worship you. To worship is to go without. To go without is death. I can't stay here anymore.

* * *

I find a rock from the playground at the zoo. I carry it to the administration building by the front entrance. It's 3 a.m. No one's around. I go around to the back of the building. I smash a window and climb in. My hand slips and my wrist slides along broken glass. Motherfucker. My pant leg catches the glass, and I rip-fall inside a room. I'm in an office. One of my superiors'. I turn my flashlight on. The room is a trap. I find the cupboard of keys and grab a set.

I'm back out of the window. I hold the keys in one hand. I head over to the monkey den. I go inside. The inmates are all asleep in their cages. Some sleep on top of one another. Some alone in corners.

The stink is worse than usual. Shit and piss and spunk and blood and vomit and tears and filth and sweat and life and death. Twenty years of it. I go to the main lock, find the key and turn it. No one moves. I'm quiet as can be.

"What the fuck do you think you're doing, asshole?"

I don't recognize the ape. He's in a separate cage.

"Who the fuck are you?" he says. "What are you in for? What did you do?"

I don't say a word. I take out my knife from my pocket and open it.

"What are you gonna do with that? Why don't you stick it up your ass?" he says.

I don't respond.

"I'm talking to you, asshole. Say something!"

His words echo in my head.

"Speak, you worthless pile of shit. Speak!"

He wants a confession. The story of my life. What can I tell him? What the fuck can I say of those mad nights? And what can I say of these nights in the zoo—with inherited prison dreams—when memories are schemes and prayers that begin something like: My dearest, my love, why didn't I die with you? I remember the rib that protrudes slightly on the left side of your body and the water-drop mole centre-high above your belly and the curls that grow, unwanted, at the back of your neck and the turn at the bridge of your nose. Vanilla skin. Sadness. And anyways, I don't feel real, you said that night at the creek. It's the thinness of your blood, diluted, that makes you say it, showing blue through your veins and pale on your skin. There's iron in pill form for women like you who lose blood easily; and the sight of it makes you sick; and the sight of a needle makes you sick. But the heart's a machine that pumps on and lives in a pit in your chest. And when your breathing is soft, alive in a cry or a moan or a laugh, it echoes out and then a pulse is easy to find. I continue to search for a beat even after it's done. But can't find yours. So quiet. Still. I'm scared to leave your body there. The ground is cold, hard. They won't believe me when I tell them we both planned to do it. Something going so wrong. One of us is still living. One of us is dead. I put a few things of yours in a box. Ballet slipper from when you were a kid. A picture from a magazine. The letter when we first planned it. Hair I cut off. At 10 a.m. it was a bus ride to any Ontario look-alike town. Bloodshot stop at a brownstone roller derby in Chatham.

Heart is in my gut. The roads are salt-stained white and the buildings are built that way on purpose—slanted, distorted. Hamilton Road South. Light a cigarette. Drink some coffee. I write the confession down. I want to suffer as you did and write as if it could be my last letter home. And the letter, a poem. And the poem, a song. Then my words might inspire my hands to do the trick. Finish it. But when they arrest me for your murder, I'm still searching for the language of our love—one to be taught to those who are dying to know what's up with us. And you are still searching for the liar in me and the killer in you and the reasons why my hands won't stop and my mouth won't stop and why my heart beats twice as fast as the next guy's—God, I swear. If you met me for the first time now—broken down, loose, and losing it—how would you come to me? Wild thoughts taking over and making me disbelieve in the things I'd always held near: love and life and you. If you met me for the first time now, would you see any trace of the person you fell for once, or the hope of a man that might be? A man not born to kill you. Would you come to me now as lover or undertaker? Would you make that suicide pact with me now? Would you draw me close and watch me raise my hands above your head?

What can I say? I can't speak now. I don't have to. The ape does all the talking.

"And you are still searching for the motherfucking liar in me and killer in you, fat fuck, and the reasons why your shitty hands won't stop and your cocksucking mouth won't stop and why your bitch heart beats twice as fast as the next guy's. God, I swear, asshole, you fucked her and strangled the little bitch. Tasted the salt from her asshole. And sweat from your groin on her thighs. You buried her body under sticks and leaves. No accident. No suicide. You backed away from doing yourself in. Vanilla skin sadness for a child hunter prick like you lost in the hunt. Fucking liar. 10 a.m. my ass. The bus ride to any Ontario look-alike town was just a lousy alibi. Bloodshot stop at a brownstone roller derby in Chatham, you bitch. You took a shit in a box. Heart is in your gut. Eat shit. Who the fuck cares? Who asked you? The roads were salt-stained white and the buildings were built that way on purpose—slanted, distorted just to hide what you did to her. Hamilton Road South, 10 a.m. despair. Who you kidding, fuck-face? Light your cigarette. Stick it up your ass. No cum, lots of sugar. Fuck you.

"All mornings as bad as this, yes. Yes, you're going to die with your dick in your mouth. The fight is in your balls. Is lost in epic battle over nothing by hot-headed barbers' sons, whose hearts and guts still burn hotter than their ocean eyes. Dead now from your unholy war with her, you'll suffer just as she does. Every time you think of her. Murder her all over again in your mind. It'll be your last letter home. Just bullshit. And the letter, just monkey shit. And the shit, a song.

"Then your words might inspire your murdering hands on her body. And your old, stupid mouth to her soul might be a retreat back to the place where you got rid of her. Why couldn't you go first?

"How simple pain is now. Who are you to fight for love? To know truth through the senses? To bind yourself with the lengths of her hair and offer tiny gifts from your blistered lips and promises that molest? May you look for love in the grave. May you rage with the war inside. May you search for her in every woman you meet. And every woman, a Mira Rose. May her body be a cage for you. The skull, ribs, and bones, its bars. Until the wounded and the strong together long for you to die. If she were to meet you for the first time now—broken down, loose, and losing it—keeping off the madness—she'd tell you to fuck off."

* * *

I open the door to the cage. Go inside. And try, with zoo dreams and the memory of Mira Rose, try to fall asleep—still—beside the others in the cage.

About the Author

Nic Labriola was born into a family for whom
laughter meant hope, and stories—survival.
Constantly risking absurdity, Nic writes stories,
poems, plays, and songs as a way to understand his
part in the human zoo. His first collection of poetry,
Naming the Mannequins, was published in 2009.
Francis and the Animals comprises fiction written
over the past 10 years, up to and including three
weeks before the manuscript went into production.
Nic teaches literature and writing at Seneca College.
He lives in Toronto.

CPSIA information can be obtained at www.ICGtesting.com
Printed in the USA
LVOW11s0955091014

407900LV00001B/5/P